BRINK

DON'T GO BACK

TO SLEEP

Men! Live Magnificently! Joy Z. Newell

~Z Newell

Library of Congress Control Number: 2015904946
Publisher: Blue Skyz Unlimited - Lexington, Kentucky USA
Front cover image: © Liz Haeberlin
Prints available upon request: info@lizimages.com
Titled "Dark Carobola"
[Back cover image by Z Newell]

Acknowledgments

I want to express my deep gratitude to Michael (Mickey) Singer, whose profound wisdom in *The Untethered Soul* was the prime inspiration for this allegory. His insights and perspective are amazing, and his presence in person radiates a joy that truly speaks to living as a spiritual human being.

I am also forever grateful to the men of the Mankind Project who have opened my heart over the past 12+ years in a way that I wish for every man on this planet.

My intention is for the journey of the main character in this story to inspire you, the reader, to quiet your mind and allow your heart to radiate with this same joy and peace of life's fullness. Each of you *is* the gift!

…and to Jackamo,
one of the wisest, most fully present,
peaceful and loving beings I know.

Gratitudes

This is my first attempt at writing a novel. It was an interesting start. The first half was all written in 'Notes' on my iPhone, until the rest began to flow and write itself. I was mainly inspired by reading Michael Singer's classic work _The Untethered Soul_, and so I first want to thank him for inspiring me to write this book. The experiences of the character in this story are by no means a full reflection of Mr. Singer's work, so I highly recommend that you create the opportunity for yourself to read that work and others of his directly.

As coincidence would have it (if there is such a thing), I was having lunch with my friend Jeffrey Weisberg while on vacation in Gainesville, Florida, and I mentioned reading _The Untethered Soul_, and starting on my own book. It turns out he knew Mickey, and that very evening I found myself listening to Mickey speaking in person at the Temple of the Universe just north of there in Alachua. I have since returned many times, and encourage you to visit there if you are ever in that area. (Visit http://www.tou.org). It is a special place, and one simply cannot visit there without leaving more attuned to their spiritual self.

It takes great dedication to consciously and intentionally lead a meaningful life, and to serve others in some manner. The characters in this story are fictitious, but are weaved from many of the people I have had the wonderful privilege of interacting with over the course of my own life adventures. I would like here to acknowledge some of these people; I am grateful for the inspiration they have given me, which has lead to my own insights, transformation, and the gift of living a full life.

Many heartfelt thanks go out to the hundreds of my Mankind Project (MKP) 'New Warrior' brothers who understand that it is worth putting forth the effort to 'change the world one man at a time'. The psychological and emotional aspects shared in this allegory are largely a result of my direct experiences and learnings from MKP. In particular, I am grateful to Geoffrey Atherton and Jeffrey Goldwasser, two of my mentors over the years who have challenged me to stretch the limits of my thinking, self-awareness and personal growth.

A few others in this brotherhood of life include my friend Rucker Wells, a passionate and creative soul on whose bathroom counter late one night I found <u>The Untethered Soul</u> lying during a visit. This fortunate occurrence–coupled with Rucker's vibrant life energy, creativity and zest for life–was a key inspiration for this book.

Another is Matt Zavadil...an incredibly alive, awake, spiritual and passionate being who inspires me by being so in tune with the rhythms of life, and sharing that with others. Finally, to Jeffrey Weisberg, another passionate individual who truly lives his mission of bringing peace into the world by bridging the communication gaps in so many challenging groups, and helping communities grow together.

There are so many other alive, passionate and awake friends who continue to inspire me at every turn! To Dennie 'Bar-Zaan' Kirtley, a long time friend who pushes through the dark with the brilliance of his trumpet; to John Fontaine, who fights for the hearts of men, to Melanie Rudolph, who laughs for the sake of laughing; and to my long-time listening friend Cai Baker, who has been willing to accept the changes within me without casting me in a static image.

Thank you, Erin Barnhill–my technical writer friend with a heart–who helped to capture some of the inconsistencies and grammatical corrections, along with coaching on how to write and 'show'. I've never had any writing classes, so her input was very helpful.

A special thanks to my neighbor Mike Meighan for taking the time to read my first draft and for being brutally honest and insightful with his feedback. His input will, hopefully, help you bond with this character and be captivated by his journey.

Thank you to Rick Broniec, who encouraged me on to publish this, and to Medicine Woman Lizette Rodriguez, who helped coach me through the process of actually publishing this book!

To my parents, Melvin and Bathsheva Weinstein...with their still sharp minds at almost 90 (as illustrated especially by my mother who graduated college at the age of 82!). For over 60 years they have loved and supported one another, and I am grateful for their constant love for me my whole life. A special thanks to my Mom for proofreading this manuscript!

To my only child's mother, Fran Welch, who has shared her love for us both consistently over time, and who understands that life in its simplest form can often bring the greatest happiness.

Last, but not least, to the two people who inspire me to go on living my life to its fullest potential. To my daughter Autumn, who continues with each challenge in her life to show me that one person committed to their personal beliefs can make a difference in the world! And to my partner and fiancée Liz Haeberlin, who is living proof that thinking positively and listening deeply–both to oneself and others–can make anything possible. Her ability to remain positive, and to visualize and manifest possibilities is incredible, and her love for me undying. Thank you, Autumn and Liz, for bringing so much love into my life and for embracing changes in your own!

To O Sensei and the art of Aikido, the peaceful martial art that embraces compassion and the flow of energy in life. To getting rid of the black hole of television in our house! To the joy of healthy, spontaneous, creative cooking, and to exercising regularly. To AnnDean Dotson's selfless giveaway of yoga in the park; to rowing in the tree house early in the morning; to hiking in nature; to meditation, touching the quiet and divine within...and, always, to living with love.

Lest I forget all of the pets of the world who provide endless loyalty, love and playfulness pure and simple to their 'people,' I thank my doggie friends, Maggie and Mango. And, of course, to Jackamo...the only non-fiction character you will find in this story!

~Z Newell

CONTENTS

ThE JOurNeY...

DON'T GO BACK TO SLEEP

The breeze at dawn has secrets to tell you.
Don't go back to sleep.

You must ask for what you really want.
Don't go back to sleep.

People are going back and forth
across the doorsill
where the two worlds touch.

The door is round and open.
Don't go back to sleep.

~Rumi

~ 1 ~

WATeR, waTer

He stood staring in amazement, still not believing that this old diner—in all its stainless steel glory—could really be out here, in the middle of nowhere. Glancing again at its single "OPEN" neon sign, he climbed the two small steps leading up to the door and pulled it open. All he could think about right now was getting some water for his raw, parched throat.

As he entered he tripped and stumbled through the doorway, falling down completely onto the linoleum floor. And there he lay, sprawled face down in embarrassment...for what seemed like an eternity....

~ 2 ~

aPPLe PiE

"You ok, Mister? Here, let me help you up," he heard the angelic voice call to him. "People always seem to be trippin' over that last stair! Ain't that somethin'?" the voice went on. "C'mon, have a seat over here. You been drinkin'?"

He stared up into a set of big beautiful blue-green eyes, barely able to focus or say anything.

"Hang on a minute. Let me get you some water," she said, as he put his head down on the counter to rest. "You look pretty tired, Mister," he heard the voice say as it moved toward him. "You hungry? Kitchen's closed, but I can let you have a piece of tomorrow mornin's apple pie. I just took it out of the oven a few minutes ago. It's on the house if you're in need. We never let anyone go hungry here in Busy. Town's too small...we all just kind of look after each other like family, know what I mean?" She paused, taking in the blank look on his face as he lifted his head to look in her direction. "Better drink some water first, Mister. You look a little pale."

He heard the sweet voice coming from somewhere outside of himself, and felt the glass being gently pushed into his hand and then lifted up to his lips. It tasted good. He must have been so dehydrated from driving under the hot prairie sun all afternoon that he was actually delirious. His mind was swimming…

I just need for this old car to hold up long enough to get me out west. It would be nice to see Mom again. I'd rather tell her in person about Dad dying, even though she doesn't seem to care anymore.

He drank down the whole thing and then heard the voice say, "You're welcome to another," as she poured him a second glass. "I'll be right back with that pie. How 'bout a little melted cheese on it? That's the way my Grannie used to serve it to us when we'd come to visit. I swear she put more love in her pies than anyone I ever knew!"

The water tasted great, and he started to come around a bit. "I'm sorry. I guess I just haven't had enough to drink today," he said as the waitress walked away, pushing her way through the swinging doors and into the kitchen to get the pie.

His throat was still parched even after two glasses of water, and he felt terribly weak. His mind wandered back down to the road from where he had been driving when… *BAM!*…that tire had blown. His head was spinning just thinking about how the sun had beaten down on him as he had struggled and fought with the four-way wrench, all the while with the continued thirst scratching at his throat…

You are so stupid! I can't believe you didn't put a couple of jugs of water in the car before you left! What if the radiator blew? You know the trip is mostly through the prairies and desert and those barren states. What made you think you could just get in the damn car and boogie off without planning? You are such a damn loser, dude!

He looked up into the mirror behind the counter, taking in his bloodshot eyes. *Man, do I look raggedy!* he thought to himself. The little curls in his light brown hair were still there. And he could see the touch of red in his sideburns that he knew he inherited from his father. Every once in a while when he got lazy about shaving, he could really see the red jump out. As for the rest of his body… it was hanging in there. He was slightly less than six feet tall and had given up on his secret wish to crack that barrier a long time ago. He wasn't in bad shape overall, although he knew that if he didn't get that extra weight in line, it could easily get out of control. *I really need to start exercising more,* flashed through his mind for the briefest of moments…

But what difference does it make? Nobody really wants me anyway. I'm just not that lovable.

He sat there, still in a daze, looking around the diner. It was as gloriously original on the inside as it was from the outside. It had old black and white pictures on the walls, a collection of license plates nailed to the area just below the cash register, menus that looked like they had been there for years and–best of all–the very stool he was sitting on, with its original orange top and glistening stainless steel base.

He knew that diners were prevalent in the Northeast and had fallen in love with them when he went to college in Massachusetts. The memory of sitting in a cold diner after midnight–then slowly warming up from eating hot lasagna and drinking coffee–was embedded in his whole body. Those experiences were so vivid and real that he was known to drive well out of his way to find anything that didn't smell of another franchise. The worst were those 'authentic diners' that had been intentionally crafted to *look* like old diners but were actually just another form of franchise in disguise. There was just something very *wrong* about that!

He had been tracking the history of diners all the way back to 1872 when they first started as horse-drawn lunch wagons. They weren't actually mass produced and referred to as 'diners' until around 1920; but he had never seen a *real* diner this far west. He knew that the railway lines started criss-crossing quite a bit out here as the land flattened out; so it seemed that someone, somehow along the way, had actually managed to move this one a bit further and plant it out here in the middle of nowhere!

He had been so excited to come across the diner when he pulled into the town that he had forgotten about both looking for a motel and his almost unbearable thirst. But now the discomfort in his throat was finally beginning to ease up a bit.

For just a moment he came out of his wandering thoughts and realized again where he was... sitting at the counter turning ever so slightly to the left, then to the right again, on this beautiful old stool. There was something about those diner stools that had always captivated him...so much so, in fact, that he had once managed to salvage one from an old diner that had closed near him in his college days. He had hauled it around for years, and finally attached it to the floor right in front of his studio work bench at the house he and Rachel had lived in. He spun a bit more, this time making a slow but complete turn...feeling the effortlessness of its circular movement beneath him. He missed his studio at that old house....

His mind flashed back to a day when he had decided to clean up his entire workshop. He had cleared the main workbench and laid out his six most recent creations of jewelry. Although painting was his main avenue of expression, he liked to dabble in various mediums from time to time. For him, it was similar to an athlete's cross-training; spending one hundred per cent of his creative time in one place seemed to lead to stagnation, so he liked to occasionally explore other modes of art as a way of getting some space and refreshing himself.

Although he wasn't quite perfectly satisfied as he stared at the most recent pieces of jewelry that he'd just finished, the critic within him had finally subsided a bit. He actually found himself in a rare *positive* mood at that moment, grateful for the energies and spirits that had brought these pieces into creation. There was a distinct yet subtle underlying thread to his creations of twisted pewter and roughly polished stone.

He was suddenly aware that–in this very moment– sitting on the diner stool thinking back to sitting at the stool by his workbench, he observed and remembered clearly how his mind had wandered off in fantasy even then. It seemed as if one of the only methods of escape from his self-torturing inner critic was either to sleep or to enter a fantasy world through his daydreaming.

As he continued to daydream, the smell of the warm pie wafted from the kitchen. He kept on with his slow rotation on the diner stool, clearly remembering his fantasy back on his own workbench stool that day, just a couple long years ago....

~ 3 ~

ArMaNi

He saw a tall, handsome, well-dressed man in an Armani suit standing before him. Walking beside the studly man on his arm was the most gorgeous woman on the planet that he could possibly imagine! She had long legs and a sleek figure, along with a unique two-tone radical haircut and a striking square jaw. And, of course, around her neck she was wearing one of his signature pewter and stone necklaces.

Two top designer magazine catalogues were vying for exclusivity to advertise his jewelry, and soon the wealth would be pouring in his direction. All of this was a result of years of staying the course and following his true passion! Just then, at the peak of his fantasy, his lovely Rachel had walked into the room. "Looks pretty neat in here for a change," she said glancing around. "It's about time." Then she spotted the pieces on the workbench. "Not bad," she said, "but none of them are even finished! Why don't you just go back out and get a real job again? You'll never make a living this way. You know we're running out of money, and you haven't had a paycheck in almost two years," she glared at him with a scowl on her face.

The irony of it was that even if the pieces had been finished, it really wouldn't have made a difference to her.

She just didn't get what the creative act was about...that his very life itself *was* living art. More than once Rachel, and sometimes others, had commented on his 'living on the edge' Bohemian lifestyle. While he had often identified with that description, there was a very different energy underneath than what his life might look like to those looking in. Although it might *appear* from the outside looking in that his life did have this gypsy-like element, something inside of him had been shifting slowly over the past few years.

Maybe it was a sign of his maturing. He had just turned thirty seven, so he was now moving away from thirty and much closer to that often referred to 'dreaded forty' on which the world seemed to place some radical significance. He felt a certain settling-in taking place and although he had nothing concrete to show for it, he felt that his potential was somehow greater than ever before. He liked to think of it just like making Jell-O. You mix the ingredients together, and then simply wait. Each time you go to the fridge and open it anxiously to see if the Jell-O is ready, it doesn't seem to be Jell-O yet. Then you get pre-occupied with something and even though you may have only stepped away for another few minutes, you suddenly remember and open the fridge again. Voila! Suddenly everything has magically congealed, as if certain elements just needed the time to fall into their respective places. In fact, his life at this time felt to him that it was not so much 'living on the edge' as if it was *on* *the brink of something greater to come…*Jell-O waiting to happen, if you will.

That's kind of ironic…Brink…just like my own name, he thought, as he sat spinning on the orange diner stool, lost in thought about those days gone by. The aroma of the apple pie heating was starting to work its way into his consciousness, as he continued to think about his own name. He had realized on more than one occasion that there were no accidents in this life. Growing up, he had never really cared for his name. In fact, he hadn't ever actually heard of anyone else named Brink, or even called that as a nickname. But over the years he had come to appreciate his name more and more as another element of his own uniqueness.

Now, turning his attention to the thought of the name Brink, he suddenly felt it resonating within him at a very deep level. It was as if the totality of him was on the brink of something huge and unknown. But this time, instead of that familiar low grade feeling of fearing the unknown that living on the edge brought with it, there was a certain indescribable peace that he was beginning to touch within himself….

~ 4 ~

BOOKMARK

He could feel the stillness rise up within him as he sat slowly spinning on the diner stool. It was an unfamiliar feeling, to say the least. Most of what he knew was a general uneasiness and dissatisfaction with himself, so this feeling of peacefulness was a stranger in his house, so to speak. *Hmmm, that was actually the same feeling I just experienced at the end of today's drive,* he noticed to himself.

He'd made the drive out west before, but had decided to take a slightly more northern route this time. He remembered reading something about Nebraska as the place "where the West begins." Since he'd lived his whole life in the Eastern part of the U.S., he thought it might be nice to start his new life out west and follow a bit of the path that the California Gold Rushers had taken. Nebraska was thinly populated with lots of open space and, quite frankly, he wasn't really up for talking to anyone these days. The voices in his head were enough to keep him occupied, and the last thing he needed was a lot of people to deal with. The open prairies seemed like a good place to mentally start his journey and maybe, just maybe, to get some respite from those voices that were continually beating him up....

What made me think that I should throw away all of my art supplies? What if I wanted to stop in the middle of the desert and paint something? I suppose it doesn't matter because most of my painting isn't that good anyway. I don't know why I ever really wasted my time with it. Maybe I should have stuck to more practical stuff a long time ago. What made me think I should give up that great, cheap space in the church basement? What if I want to go back? What if I run out of money and can't buy more supplies, or more gas to finish this damn trip? This old car will probably give out pretty soon anyway. Now the A/C is gone...man, it was so hot today! Why am I going out there anyway? I've been to the Burning Man festival so many times...I'm probably just wasting more time avoiding making something happen in my life. I should have just ended it back there with my dad's old Winchester rifle instead of fighting with that damned flat tire...geez, I'm not even forty yet and I could barely even change that sucker. I know it's that extra ten pounds I put on that gets me out of breath so quick, but who gives a damn about how I look anyway? I'm done with girlfriends and I can't afford hookers...hell, I can't even afford regular dating. It costs more money than I ever have. And who ever came up

*with the custom that the guy needs to pay
all the time anyway? I'd like to shoot the
person who started that ridiculous trend!
Even if I could afford it, I just screw things
up most of the time with women anyway,
so what's the point of it all?*

But then at some point, as the drive wore on, he began to *notice* that the voices were beating him up. The difference was a subtle one, and he wasn't quite sure what to make of it. Somehow, he found himself *watching* the messages beating on him in a way that was different from *listening* to the voices themselves. As annoying–and sometimes even terrifying–as all of his inner talk was, the part of him that *noticed* those other parts did not contain the same feelings that the voices themselves brought up in him. There was a certain calmness of this *watching himself* listening to the voices in his head that was very different from his actual *reactions* to the messages. So how could it be that the same 'him' who was tormented daily by those inner messages–with all of their accompanying anxiety–could simultaneously feel calmness and peace? Which of those directly opposing states was actually 'him'? Who exactly was Brink Simmer anyway? And, as if those questions weren't complicated enough, how could he possibly find peace when those moments were just a *glimmer* in between the damned barrage of never-ending negative thoughts that he kept beating himself up with?

On the drive, he had decided to 'bookmark' those thoughts. 'Bookmarking' was something he had learned from his mother a long time ago. When he would ask a question of her–such as where his father had gone away to–she would respond with, "Let's bookmark that and talk about it later." Looking back now, he realized that this was simply an expression she used to avoid answering his questions…because more often than not, "later" never came. Yet he had adopted 'bookmarking' as a method for mentally making a note of things that he himself wanted to remember and come back to later to explore. Sometimes he did, and sometimes he didn't, but bookmarking at least gave him a temporary feeling of closure around things.

Brink sat at the diner counter slowly coming to consciousness. He had no idea how long he'd been sitting there just thinking…thinking…thinking. *How long does it actually take to have a thought? And how many thoughts there are at any given time!* he noted to himself. He once researched this very question, and had learned that experts estimated people to have anywhere between 2000-3300 thoughts per hour. That was as many as sixty to eighty thousand thoughts per day. No wonder he felt like he was going crazy!

He could hear the waitress singing from the kitchen as she finished working on readying the pie. *Whoever heard of putting cheese on apple pie anyway?* he thought, as he continued to relax and swivel back and forth on the stool. It was almost hypnotic, and his mind wandered back

again to the place he had stayed in for safe harbor this
past year since his big breakup with Rachel....

~ 5 ~

hIdiNg OuT

He had been living in the basement of an old church that a musician buddy of his had somehow managed to buy and convert into an amazing recording studio. The basement was a small apartment that an occasional out of town band would stay in…not very big, but cheap enough for him to handle with the small savings he had been stretching out. When there was no recording going on, he would sometimes use the main sanctuary recording space to paint. He had his art, and that was all that kept him going now that his corporate life work world and personal love life had petered out. He didn't care about giving up the fancy house… although he did miss the Corvette that he used to cruise to work in. As he reminisced over what was undoubtedly his favorite car ever, he found himself pining over it. *Man could that car hug the road!* he thought, with his face breaking out into a big smile.

Brink admitted to himself that he enjoyed that car and had secretly wanted it for years, just as most people want all kinds of things. People consumed themselves, in his humble opinion, with the desire to have more and more of everything. More cars, more clothes, more vacations…all of it. Yeah, there was nothing wrong with that. It's just that ultimately those things weren't really that important to him.

He valued having his *time* more than anything. A friend of his had once told him that in a lot of ways he was much wealthier than most people because of his lifestyle and abundance of free time. Sure, he needed some money to get by, just like most. He managed somehow...waiting tables now and then, occasionally selling some of his art or doing odd job house painting work.

There were definitely pros and cons to hiding out in his church studio. But at least now he was painting for *himself;* it hadn't always been that way. When he had 'sold out' to do the corporate gig and fancy life style, he had promised himself that he would hold on to both his art and going to the Burning Man festival as often as possible. That festival had to be one of the most creative and unique gatherings on the planet–at least in his humble opinion–and it rejuvenated him in a way that nothing else seemed to.

Working on his art and going to Burning Man were the only two things that really brought him to life. He had hated being in the corporate world, even though it brought in the big bucks, made Rachel happy, and stabilized some of the other chaos in his life. He had convinced himself, over and over, that all would be fine, so long as he held onto his art. So he continued to plug away at painting and the few other mediums that he dabbled in, such as his occasional pieces of jewelry art.

At a certain point while he was still painting as a side activity to his job, he actually felt that he had almost perfected the fine details of his technique. He was smitten with the Photorealism style that had begun in the late 1960's and early 70's. He had painted a series of diners recreated from photographs snapped here and there with a Brownie Polaroid camera that he had bought at a yard sale years before. His focus had been to perfectly reproduce the details of each photographic image on canvas. It was really just a matter of taking the tedious time to copy the image exactly; in some ways it almost felt like cheating to him. Yet he must have touched something in his audience—at least that's what he told himself—because his paintings began to suddenly sell…and for more than he had ever imagined!

The ironic thing was that he needed the money less in his life than ever because of the money he made doing corporate sales training work; and yet he had sold more of those perfectly detailed paintings than any other style he had been through in search of his personal signature niche! *What's up with that?* he wondered. Since art was supposedly a reflection of life, it appeared that the popularity of perfectionism was an indicator of what most people wanted...or perhaps it was just a reflection of those who had the extra money to spend.

But as popular as his work had become on the local scene, underneath he felt that it was not the art that spoke to his soul. So although the surface detail and style was impeccable, there was something beneath all of it that left him with an uneasy feeling. It was almost as if the surface details were covering up a hidden canvas that was screaming to reveal itself. Looking back on his painting and other art from his corporate years, he suddenly understood that everything had not been as it seemed at the time. His perfectionist phase–which he had thought at the time finally marked his 'arrival' to the creative process–had in retrospect really been the polar opposite. Underneath his willingness to sit still and master the fine details in his painting was a pent up energy that was force feeding this perfectionism. He didn't really want to funnel his wild energy and enthusiasm for life into this myopic, technical form of perfectionism. What he really wanted was to *experience* the wildness of life and put *that* on the canvas!

So while the upside of hiding out was that no people bothered him, the downside was that–with all of his alone time–the voices seemed to grow far worse than ever before. With no distractions from the outside world, the voices and their messages turned inward and followed him everywhere he went, like a swarm of bees; they simply wouldn't let him clear his mind and leave him with even the smallest bit of peace. Most people wanted fancy cars, boats and possessions. All Brink really wanted was some peace of mind, literally. *Is that so much to ask, really?* was all he had said himself at that time, and now again sitting here....

~ 6 ~

WICkeR iNVItaTioN

"Here you go, Mister," the waitress said, placing the hot pie topped with melted cheese in front of him. "Want some coffee or a glass of milk to wash that down?"

He looked up to see those sweet blue-green eyes staring down at him again. Not that he was looking, mind you. He was still on the path of being relationship free and wanting to stay there. But if a person *had* to be looking into a pair of eyes, these were certainly a more than beautiful set! They seemed to change from blue to green then back again as he looked up into them.

And as if her eyes were not enough in and of themselves, the rest of her slim, shapely figure was certainly not to be overlooked. He guessed her to be maybe thirty at most. She wasn't the voluptuous type with large breasts and exaggerated hips...one of those who bounced around flaunting her assets, seeking to attract attention at every turn. No, there was something very subtle, yet defined, about both her shape and her presence itself. Her breasts were understated but most definitely noticeable under the plain white T-shirt she was wearing. And her well-worn jeans fit her tight bottom like a leather glove. *Understated, if anything,* thought Brink, as he looked back at her. *This is not a*

25

woman trying to catch a man. This is just a woman, plain and simple.

"Or do you just want another glass of water?" she asked in her soft, lulling voice. After getting no verbal response from him, she just continued on, saying "Let me get you another drink. You still look a little out of it."

"Um, yes, water sounds good, thank you, Miss..."

"Olivia", she replied.

"Yes, thank you, Olivia. I guess I didn't drink enough today.…I'm actually feeling a little weak. I've been on the road all day and haven't eaten much either. This pie sure is delicious!" He took another bite then asked, "The motel I saw didn't have a sign lit up. Is it still open?"

"Well, to tell you the truth, old Mr. Sefcik died last year and we haven't really had anyone take it over just yet."

"Would that have been 'Hugo' that I saw on the sign back down the road?" he asked. Brink clearly remembered both the homemade sign he had seen posted at the edge of town and his thoughts at the time…

WELCOME TO BUSY

POPULATION: ~~72~~ 71

WE LOVE + MISS HUGO!

As he passed it, he had thought:

Hmmm...BUSY? What in the hell kind of name is that for a town? Well, I suppose I can deal with a few of those 71 people if I have to, but I'd rather not talk to anyone right now if I have a choice about it. And who the heck is Hugo that he's so damn important anyway? Must be someone's idea of a joke...I don't get it, but that's just par for the course....

Guess you're just not a funny guy....

Brink recalled–as he had been observing his own thinking process–that his 'observer' had noted:

Why is it that sometimes my voice talks to me as YOU and sometimes it's just I/ME thinking? I suppose whether it's 'I' or 'You' is all a moot point; it's getting the voices to STOP that's the real problem. I just wish they would GO AWAY and give me some damn peace! I don't know how much longer I can stand this!

That was the last thought he could recall having, as he had eased into the little crossroads town looking for a drink of water and a motel room to crash for the night. And that was when he had spotted the diner....

"Well, I'll be!" he heard the waitress squeal with delight, upon hearing Brink comment on the sign. "Someone actually noticed my sign!" she said, breaking into a brilliant smile. Brink snapped out of his thought trance and smiled to himself, amused by how genuinely delighted she seemed at her sign work being noticed by someone. In the same moment, he realized that he had once again spaced out and let his thinking take him completely away from being in the moment with her.

"I tell you what," she continued, "I've got a wicker couch on my porch that you're welcome to sleep on. It's not as comfortable as the motel beds…but like I said, we try to make sure folks get what they need around here."

"That's very kind of you, Miss Olivia, but I really couldn't do that. I'll just sleep in the back seat of my car. Thank you though," he responded.

"Now don't be silly!" she insisted in response to his turning down her invitation. "It's been over a hundred degrees during the days almost all week, and the nights don't seem like they've been much better," she declared." I'm sure that stuffy old car couldn't possibly be as comfortable as a couch on a screened porch with the breeze blowing through. I can even put an extra fan out for you. Gimme just about five minutes to finish closing up and we can head over that way."

She turned to walk away, and he couldn't help but be drawn to how her hips moved. It wasn't a blatant swagger…just enough shift from side to side to make it clear that she was womanly. He guessed her height to be about 5'7" or so…and a great complement to his own 5'11". Brink thought to himself:

If I were five years younger and eight to ten pounds lighter passing through here, I'd probably go after her for a one-night stand...but I guess those days are past me now....

Just then, as if to be reading his mind, she looked back at him over her shoulder and added, "But don't be getting any ideas, Mister. I may seem to some like a pushover, but I've sent more than a few men scurrying off looking down the barrel of my grandpa's shotgun."

Brink smiled and shook his head. "No worries here, Miss Olivia. Even if that was what I was after, this body's got to get some serious sleep right now. I'll feel lucky if I can even make it as far as that porch of yours. I appreciate your hospitality...by the way, my name's Brink."

"OK, then, Mr. Brink. I'll be right back and we'll head over. It's just a short walk from here." Then she pushed through the swinging doors to the kitchen, and that was the last thing that Brink could remember....

~ 7 ~

waVeS oN tHe PLaiNs

He found himself in his car again, cruising across the hot plains. Some called it the desert; others, who had been further west where not even prairie grasses grew, might disagree. Desert or not, it was hot and he was getting thirstier and thirstier. But he couldn't stop now; they were following him. As he sped up he saw several fresh streams of water by the side of the road...natural springs to quench his parched throat. But he couldn't risk stopping, not even for a few minutes. They had been following him for years, as long as he could remember, in fact. It didn't matter where he went, they followed him...in the daytime or at night, at work or when he tried to relax...when he painted...even when he made love. There were waves and waves of them...and they just kept coming....

The waves seemed to be getting bigger all the time. Here he had thought that he could escape them...perhaps by going west and into the desert where he could clear his mind for once. He looked up in his rear view mirror and saw the next one...it was a huge *wave of thoughts* about to come crashing down on him. He pressed down on the accelerator, driving faster and faster, until the car gently lifted up off the dusty road and into the sky…away, away at last! His car was flying amidst the clouds, in and out of them, with glimmers of blinding sunshine as he cruised effortlessly over the landscape below.

He looked down to see the Nebraska panhandle's thousands and thousands of miles of wind-shaped dunes and prairie grasses, the endless sand and tumbleweed, with an occasional turkey or buffalo and every now and then an old house or barn suspended in the middle of the vast emptiness. Then a small clustering of buildings appeared where two desolate roads intersected, and he eased the car in for a smooth landing in front of the diner, with its lonely yet inviting lights….

The waves of thought kept washing over him like the cool breeze as the night passed…Rachel, his unfinished art, the man in the Armani suit, his dad, the Corvette…then back to sitting in the diner again, reliving those moments in time. Aaah…the diner…the pie…the waitress…the water! *"Better drink some water first, Mister,"* he heard her voice echo again, as the cool glass was pressed into his hand and lifted to his lips.

So now he was thinking…no, *dreaming about thinking*…about his own thoughts from the past. Layers upon layers of thoughts; just how many layers were there? It reminded him of a bizarre movie he had once seen. And now here he was, tossing in his dream state, yet actually *aware of himself dreaming.*

He was so deeply lost in the layers that he couldn't tell

what was real from what he was dreaming…and yet the whole time–even as he tasted that pie again–he continued to somehow be *aware* of the fact that he was *watching* this entire series of images in his very own dream. The 'bookmark'…there it was again!

As the images and thoughts floated past him, he felt something wet and cold on the back of his hand…then something soft pushing against him. This time it was different from the feel of the cool hard glass of water being pressed into his hand. It was a soft, cold, insistent pressing, pushing against the back of his hand in the gentlest of ways.

He slowly opened his eyes to see a cat looking over at him. It was perched on the little glass table next to the wicker couch he was suddenly aware of lying on, with his arm drooping gently over the table. The cat continued insistently pushing first his nose and then his head into the back of Brink's hand, over and over–as if wanting something–until Brink finally came awake enough to realize that the cat was simply trying to scratch the back of its own head. It was one of those orange tabby cats…ginger cats as some people referred to them. The cat stretched himself out. How perfect he looked! He had a gradual shift in color from the solid orange of his body, which then blended into raccoon-like rings of orange and white, ending in a white tip with just a touch of subtle, barely detectable color at the end.

Brink looked at the cat's perfectly formed face, with its nose that had been rubbing up against him, the long whiskers, tiger-striped forehead and near perfect ears. His left ear had just a touch of a tattered edge, from where he must have been in a tussle with some other animal, thought Brink. Then he peered into the cat's intensely green luminescent eyes with their long narrow vertical black cat eye slits, and he reached up behind its ears to finally answer the cat's "scratch me" call. The cat let out a soft purr which seemed to emanate from the depths of its whole being. It seemed so relaxed and peaceful, wanting so little–just a bit of scratching behind its ears–to bring it to this full and happy, almost blissful state…at least that's how Brink imagined it to be feeling.

He opened his own eyes a bit more and looked around the screened porch to see the rest of the wicker furniture. An extra wide, old oak porch swing was suspended from the ceiling at the other end, with a backdrop of green from a lone tree next to the house, along with baskets of purple flowers hanging throughout the porch. Gradually he began to remember the waitress from the diner bringing him there and laying him on the couch to sleep. It was almost as if he had been drunk the night before. He barely remembered anything about getting there…although he seemed to remember *everything* that had been going through his head last night, as well as the lucid dream[1] that had delivered him to this present moment.

As his eyes came back to the deeply purring cat, he spotted a small handwritten note on top of the scratched glass table top next to him:

Make yourself at home. There's
coffee in the kitchen or come on over
to the diner for some breakfast
...on the house if need be
~Olivia

Olivia. Brink thought about her name and realized he had never met an Olivia before. In fact, as his thoughts wandered back to the few brief glimpses of her at the diner, something inside told him that he had never met anyone quite like her. He had barely seen or spoken with her except for just a few quick exchanges. But who could he remember–at least outside of the extraordinary hospitality of folks at Burning Man–that would just open their home to a stranger?

Burning Man[2] was all about sharing. People came each year just to share with each other…everything from food and water to entertainment and laughter and a plethora of wild and crazy experiences…all with the best of intentions. Where else on the planet would 50,000 people show up and haul every bit of supplies–including water–into the middle of the desert…just to share and celebrate life and creativity?

Yet here was a perfect stranger willing to share food and shelter for no apparent reason at all. Ordinarily, in the world in which he was used to living, Brink would be almost suspicious of ulterior motives. But he recalled the shotgun warning she had given him and ruled out that type of motive on her part. No, there was something very different about her that he had not come across before with other people in his life. He couldn't quite put his finger on it....

~ 8 ~

SELLING OUT

Although the wicker couch was fairly comfortable, Brink's back was still sore from the long ride the day before. One of the springs in the car's seat had popped long before he ever even inherited the car; it was tolerable on short drives, but the long distance trip had turned this small irritant into a growing ache slowly working its way up his back. Once again, his negativity and regrets reared their ugly voice…

> *I never should have gotten rid of my 'vette!*
> *Not much room for storage but, man, were*
> *those bucket seats comfortable!*

He just couldn't stop thinking about life in those corporate days when–at least on some level–things seemed to have gone his way for a while. Everything appeared to be at a peak; he was making great money, things with Rachel were simple and fun, and for just a little while he was living like a high roller…until he decided to walk away from it all. Well, at least that's the story that he liked to tell himself.

Truth be told, they had "eliminated his position"… corporate speak for firing him. Technically, they told him they had actually "merged the position with another" and were actively seeking applicants. But "he just wasn't a good fit" for the revised position. Corporate speak...again. He remembered the voices ringing in his ears back then as clear as a bell:

> *You did it again, Bro! They just don't like you. You're not good enough for them. You just don't belong here–or probably anywhere–with people. You're not worth a dime to anyone!*

He stayed angry and bitter about it for quite some time, with thoughts of getting an attorney and maybe even filing some form of wrongful action suit. But after settling down a bit, he realized that he really wasn't entirely the victim in this situation. Underneath it all he knew he had a pretty powerful passive-aggressive side; and he was quite masterful at using it. Allowing someone to see that they were rubbing him the wrong way and affecting him was not his style. Instead, he would quietly probe back at them, artfully undermining them until their own seeds of self-doubt began to sprout. There was just no way that he would give others the satisfaction of seeing that they were hurting him in some way. That would really be like letting them see they had won. No. Suing them would be just like that, even if he did win.

The reality was that this passive-aggressive side had contributed to his downfall. He had this "king killer" in him, as he had heard it called...the side of him where he simply *had to be right*. Some of the programs and policies in the company simply did not make sense to him. He knew there were more effective ways to implement certain things, but he wasn't willing to play the long, drawn out power games of going through all those political channels to do it. He didn't have the patience for all that crap. So occasionally when his passive-aggressive element boiled over, it came out as blatant criticism of his supervisors in open situations. He simply would not–in fact, he actually *could not*– hold back from expressing himself and cutting them down in front of others. The bottom line for him was that he simply had no fear in expressing what he really thought when others pushed his buttons. He heard the voice again loud and clear:

> *Things were going along fine and then you just had to open your mouth and trip over the last stair. Are you ever going to stop setting yourself up for the big fall?*

Maybe it was 'emotional intelligence' that he was deficient in. He had read up on all of that when he was in college, so he had the *awareness* of how to play the games...when to shut up and suck up...when to chum with the others to be more acceptable, and all that went with 'emotional smarts' and surviving amidst the tribe. If he put his mind to it, he could probably do great on the *Survivor* TV series...the one where they tossed an unlikely mix of people together on an island somewhere until they slowly voted one another off the show.

What it really all boiled down to was whether or not he *wanted* to play. Truth be told, he didn't. Yeah, there was a part of him that dug the fancy car he had been driving, the new motorcycle in his garage, an occasional trip to the Bahamas with Rachel and all the other fun stuff. But the bottom line was that he just didn't *want* to play the games. Maybe he just never had the team player thing in him. He had played sports all through high school and done well…until he realized toward the end that his heart was just not in it, and he had walked away from it all.

He glanced at Olivia's note about the coffee and, although he felt a little odd walking into this stranger's home, he saw that the porch door was already partly open… so he pushed it open the rest of the way. It let out a slow c-r-e-a-k just as the cat slipped by him. The cat turned and looked at him, almost as if to say, *"Follow me"*…which Brink proceeded to do. The cat led him straight to the kitchen.

He could smell the coffee, but looked around and didn't see a coffee maker anywhere. Then he spotted one of those old wooden square coffee grinders like the kind you see in museums or antique shops. Next to it was some kind of quilted thing; it looked like a pillow or soft dome with a little handle at the top. He slowly lifted it to see a beautiful handcrafted pottery teapot underneath. *Definitely coffee, not tea,* he thought as he breathed more deeply to take in the wonderful aroma. *Do people really stop and grind their coffee by hand?* Just then the cat jumped up at the end of the counter; actually, it almost seemed as if he *floated* gracefully onto the counter...and Brink's eyes fell on a cup and some sugar set just off to the side. He helped himself, just as the note had said. *"There's fresh goat milk in the fridge,"* said another little note right next to it.

After he had mixed what he somehow knew was one of the freshest cups of coffee he could possibly hope for, he decided to head back to the porch. *After all,* he thought to himself, *I'm a stranger in someone's home and I shouldn't be poking around here.* In his mind he knew that proper social behavior told him he didn't belong there; yet in his body he felt a strange sense of comfortableness that didn't seem to match what he *thought* he should be feeling....

dARk CArOBOLA

As Brink passed back through the living room he glanced over at the wall to see an incredible set of three paintings hanging there. They weren't like anything he could ever remember painting himself. He was mesmerized by them, not quite sure what he was *supposed* to be looking at, but somehow seeing a blend of calming images rising out of each canvas. They were continuous as a set, yet separate from each other. The one in the middle was larger and clearly dominant, while the outer two seemed to frame and reflect it in some manner. On the surface of the center painting was a blend of bright whites and yellows easing into greens, with moving streaks of black washing through it all. It was as if he were looking into some deep reflection of his own consciousness. It had a bright, optimistic quality to it, yet underneath a deep-seated darkness rose up to greet the optimism. After an eternity of taking those pieces in, he came out of his trance and looked around to realize that there was art everywhere in the room.

On his first pass through, he had been following the cat, which seemed to have very intentionally and deliberately led him to the coffee in the kitchen. So he had passed right through this room not really noticing its contents. As he looked around more carefully, he saw that there were many paintings of similar–yet very different–styles. But there was also an abundance of sculpture and other clay-fired pieces. Most of them had that same cracked smoky look that he knew came from a raku firing kiln, just as the teapot in the kitchen had been. Scattered amongst all of the paintings and clay pieces were some of the most beautifully kept plants he had ever seen, including a few gorgeous orchids and several well-trimmed miniature bonsai plants. *What an alive room!* was all he could think to himself.

He savored each sip of his coffee as he made his way around the room for several more sets of eternities, lost in each of the uniquely vivid paintings that hung on the parlor walls. Then suddenly from behind him he heard the screen porch door creak open and in walked Olivia holding two foil-covered plates in her hands.

"Looks like Jackamo showed you to the coffee. He's such a good little man to have around the house," she declared. "Brought you some hot food!" the sweet voice continued right on. "Glad to see you got to sleep in and rest up. You sure didn't look very good last night… must've gotten yourself some heat stroke or somethin' driving through the plains like that. Don't you know you're supposed to drink at least a gallon of water a day?"

"Well, I wasn't really thinking about it, I guess," Brink replied, glancing again at the plates in her hands and realizing how hungry he suddenly felt.

She spotted his glance and said, "C'mon. Let's go sit down in the kitchen so you can enjoy this before it gets cold," and then disappeared as quickly as she had appeared.

He followed her into the kitchen and sat at the table, watching her as she poured herself a cup of coffee, then continuing his gaze as she walked over to freshen his cup. Somehow it seemed as if serving others was just second nature to her. "Go on and have at that food. Don't be bashful. I don't want you collapsing on me again like you just about did last night. I barely got you back here and settled onto that couch. You sleep OK?"

Brink took a few bites of breakfast, then a few more, feeling grateful for the nourishment his body was already beginning to absorb. "Yes, just fine, thank you," he responded. He thought about telling her about the almost bizarre mix of dreams and self-awareness running through them that he had experienced, but decided to leave that for his own future ponderings.

"Aren't you going to join me?" he asked, pointing at the second foil-covered plate.

"No, silly. I'm good. That plate is the last slice of that apple pie you had last night…you seemed to enjoy it, so I thought I'd bring you another piece."

"Not sure what you put in that pie, but it was definitely one of the most delicious pies I can ever remember eating," he said, as he continued to almost devour the food in front of him.

"Oh, it's just an ol' pie, that's all…but I always use my grandma's secret ingredient when I cook."

"What's that?" asked Brink with a slight quizzical expression.

She smiled, hesitating just a bit, and then said simply, "Love."

Her response was straightforward, but it somehow surprised Brink.

> *Love? What in the hell is this woman talking about? Flour, sugar, eggs, apples and whatever else goes in there, sure. But don't give me any of this hocus-pocus stuff. There is something about this gal that is a bit off the charts…can't quite put my finger on it…*

Brink squirmed just a bit in his seat, silently focusing on the plate in front of him.

"You'd best slow down a bit with that food, or you might just find yourself choking if you're not careful," Olivia said to him gently.

"I don't mean to be rude eating so fast," he replied. "It's just that, well, I guess I really didn't eat much on the road yesterday except some chips and snacks and…well, this just *tastes so good!*" he proclaimed.

"At the pace you're eating, I'd be surprised if you actually even *tasted* it," she responded. "But I'm very glad that you are enjoying it. I just don't want to have to do the Heimlich maneuver on you from choking," she said laughingly.

Brink slowed his pace down and gradually finished the plate of food, scraping the last of the tasty morsels onto his fork. *She's right,* he thought to himself,

> *...the food really does taste better when I slow down to enjoy it. She certainly doesn't hesitate to speak her mind, but in a different kind of way than I'm used to. Seems like she can express herself so clearly and simply, but somehow I'm not getting all defensive. I mean, I'm so used to arguing with people, but there's something so honest about the way she speaks what's on her mind that it's hard to take it personally. I wish everyone I met was as easy to talk with as her....*

In that very moment, Brink once again felt a calmness come over him. Even more interestingly, he suddenly *noticed* himself calming down. After the silence had settled, he looked at his empty plate, pushed his chair back from the table, and glanced up at her standing by the counter. Finally–after what seemed like quite a long silence had passed–he said, "Can I ask you something? It's about those paintings in there. Did you paint them?"

"Well I'll be!" was her response, almost startling him.

Immediately the voice in Brink's head started second guessing his own simple question.

Did I offend her in some way? Was I inappropriate? Geez, Brink, can't you even ask a simple question without it coming out wrong?

There it was again, right on cue…the voice of self-doubt looming up to fill his head. Finally, he looked at her like a small child and offered, "Did I say something wrong?"

Before his self-critic could go any further, he heard her laugh and reply with the sweetest of smiles, "Not at all! It's just that I was beginning to wonder if you would   ever   ask   *any*   questions!"

"What do you mean by that?" he asked, with somewhat of a puzzled look on his face.

"You see, Grams…that's what I always called my Grandma Violet before she died a few years back…"

There was suddenly a pause in the air as Olivia stared out the kitchen window for a moment. "I keep all those beautiful violets out on the porch to remind myself of her every time I come into the house," she continued, pulling her gaze back into the room and looking toward Brink once again. "Anyway, Grams told me to always be a bit wary of strangers if they start asking you a lot of questions right off the bat. But you, Mr. Brink, you haven't asked a *single* question since you inquired about the motel at the diner last night…well, not up until just a few minutes ago, that is…."

"It's just Brink...not 'Mr.' by the way. So..." he repeated the question hesitantly, "*are* the paintings and all that art work in there yours?"

"Just the paintings are mine," she said. All the sculpture and pottery was Gram's. But she's the one who got me started on painting when I used to come and visit. She pretty much raised me since I was fourteen, when my folks were killed in a car accident."

"Oh, I'm sorry to hear that," replied Brink, suddenly flashing on his own upbringing. It wasn't exactly the same because his father hadn't actually died, but he had pretty much been raised just by his Mom after his father had left them.

"It's OK. Everything worked out just like it was supposed to, I guess," she went on. "I couldn't imagine ever being raised by anyone as loving and wise as Grams. In the ten or so years I lived with her before she died, she gave me everything I needed, and taught me everything I would ever need to know about living in this world. This was her and Grandpa Tomas' house. He was Czech and came over from the old country back in 1945. He was still a young man, in his late 20's, I think. Somehow he knew enough to get out of living over there and sure enough, just a short time later in 1948, the Communists seized power.

"Tomas means 'twin' in Czech, by the way," she explained. "Grams told me that his twin had died during his mom's childbirth, so they named him Tomas to carry the energy of both of them. He was making his way west

to California–like a lot of people chasing their dreams–
when he met Grams and…well, I guess they just kind of
fell in love. He died almost twenty years ago. I really
miss him. I used to hang around his workshop out back
when we would come to visit. He was a very handy
man…he even showed me a little bit about how to weld
one time. I was barely ten, but he treated me just like a
grown person."

Brink couldn't help but feel a tinge of sadness as he
watched Olivia glance toward the window again. Her
short, bright red hair looked a bit uneven in places, as if
she might have simply cut it herself with a scissors. As
she turned back toward him, he noticed that her face,
unlike many typical redheads, was freckle-free, and her
complexion was robust and healthy.

"They had a difficult but wonderful life together until
he just one day up and had a big ol' heart attack," Olivia
continued to tell him. "Grams told me once that she
ached for a long time after that…until I came along one
day about four years later when my folks died. They were
crossing the train tracks in Lincoln when their car stalled
out and they were both killed. That's where we'd been
living since I was about five, because there really were no
schools out here for me. My mama wanted real bad for
me to get an education so I could move on up and out of
this town, as she used to say."

"Next thing you know Grams was raising me, and I've
pretty much been here ever since. She passed on about
five years ago…left me the house, all her beautiful

sculptures, her pottery wheel and kiln, and lots of love in my heart…"

Olivia went on for five or ten minutes, sharing more of her grandmother's pieces of wisdom with Brink. Clearly her grandmother had been a very wise woman. Finally, she turned to look back at the cat, which seemed to be sitting there watching and listening to them.

"Your paintings…" he continued. "I've never really seen anything quite like them. Those three on the big wall…can you tell me about those?"

"Oh, you mean the Dark Carobola? You like those?" responded Olivia.

"Carobola? Is that a word?" asked Brink.

"Well, it is now!" she laughed refreshingly. "If I can create the painting, why not create the name, too? To tell you the truth, I really don't have a whole lot to say about any of them…they just sort of come out of me from time to time. I painted those when I was picnicking down by the Niobrara River one day. Anyway, there's not much I can tell you about them; they should just speak for themselves. Did they have anything to say to *you*?"

Wow! was all Brink could think to himself, somewhat dumbfounded. His mind flashed to the myriads of paintings and hours of self-torture he had brought upon himself anguishing over his paintings, his intentions, the surface and hidden meanings, what he projected others might say or think about each work, and on and on….

Does it really have to be this difficult? was the thought that rose up in Brink's mind just then. In his gut, he knew that there must be something *underneath* all of this that would help him better understand why his painting–and his life–seemed to be so tormented. *Couldn't anything just be simple, rather than layers of hidden meanings?* he asked himself. In a strange sort of way, it reminded him of the Dark Carobola....

~ 10 ~

uNDeRcUrrEnts

Brink's painting was really the *only* thing he had to call his own after he had gotten 'ejected' –as he sometimes thought of it–from both the corporate world and from his relationship with Rachel. He had worked *so* hard and deliberately at creating pieces of significance that most of the time they seemed to end up…well…too cluttered. Thinking about it at that moment, he realized just how hard he had been trying to fit everything of significance into his work, rather than just relaxing and letting it flow. Now here was Olivia–a person with no formal art training–and all she seemed to do to create these amazing pieces was to "just let it come out from time to time," as she had described it.

It occurred to Brink that perhaps that was part of the core problem with so much of his life. Maybe he simply had been trying *too* hard to make all the pieces fit together. It was clear, looking back, that neither Rachel nor the corporate world had really been a very good fit for who he was. So how had he gotten there in the first place?

He was pulled into the traditional business life at Rachel's prodding, and by an introduction to her uncle who had placed him in the sales department at his company. He had survived–and actually thrived– in that environment for quite a few years until he was ultimately fired. At first he had felt anger and great injustice. *Who do they think they are? What right do they have to do this?* had been the repeated mantra in his head for months. Losing his job had led to the further unraveling of his relationship with Rachel, contributing to her eventually walking out on him.

Looking back now, it was all really quite a relief. Yes, it was an uncomfortable, somewhat embarrassing, and even tumultuous time. After losing his job, their money situation had turned bleak in less than a year when his savings had run out. Although Rachel was still working, they had gotten sucked into the big house with a big mortgage syndrome, and it all had become overwhelming very quickly. Their financial struggles and suffering created lots of stress for both of them; it had been difficult times, but somehow they had managed to stick together for a few more very long years. But the truth was that the *real* 'suffering' was what he had experienced trying to fit who he was into the job itself and into their relationship as well.

He had been smitten by her, and vice versa. He was living the life of the Bohemian artist when they first met, and she was the sexy, successful businesswoman. Each had been attracted to the other's world, perhaps as an escape from their own individual worlds, or maybe out of some kind of twisted need to complete a part of each of them that was missing. She seemed to crave his 'wild man' creative, raw energy side and his refusal to be cast in a mold or told how to live by anyone. And he must have secretly wanted to be associated with success and being highly organized, finding his coupling with her satisfying in some way.

They were a bit of an enigma, for sure. When they showed up at a party, she would laughingly introduce him as her "artist in residence." "Isn't he adorable?" she would laughingly ask, as if showing off her new little puppy dog. Their collection of 'friends', if you wanted to call them that, was a hybrid of socialites who seemed to find Brink a fascinating conversation piece, along with some of his own artist friends who never seemed to stop questioning him about "What was up?" with the two of them anyway.

She was sexy indeed and–at least at first impression– seemed quite self-confident. Not only had he been attracted to those aspects of her life that were missing in his own, but he had somewhat willingly followed her into her world of business as well. After that came the many temptations that the money from his newfound corporate job had brought...the brand new Corvette they had driven to the factory in Bowling Green, Kentucky to buy, their trips to St. John and the myriads of other material treats they indulged in.

What made me think...that I belonged there or could possibly fit in? was all he could ask himself, thinking back on it now. Underneath it all, a part of him had known that none of his personal values even remotely resembled that world. How could he possibly fit the ideas, hopes, dreams, and values that had shaped his thinking and belief system up to that point in his life into *her* world?

Did I really do all of that for her? his little voice asked him. The answer that came to him was a resounding *No.* There was, as always, more underneath that it had taken a long time for him to get a glimpse of. His father—just before walking out on his wife and son— had told Brink to "make something" of himself. He knew he didn't want to end up like his father, who had turned into a useless alcoholic in the end.

Between his subconscious motivations to please his absent father and not become like him, and Rachel's life of material temptations, he had quietly tormented himself...trying to get his *internal* thoughts and belief systems to line up with the values and behaviors that went along with that *external* corporate world.

That was no easy task! The first step had been the initial bending of his behavior to essentially pretend— from the 'outside looking in'—that he actually fit into that environment. The fancy clothes that Rachel had decked him out in had felt like a fun game that he was willing to step into to make her happy. He could see her primping him in his mind's eye, not only for work but for those wonderful corporate parties that she lived to attend with him.

None of that really felt like a big deal. In fact, he sort of enjoyed 'acting the part.' He told himself that it was just another form of living art. Acting was something that he had always been fascinated by but had never really tried during his academic years, so why not step into it now for a bit?

The really difficult part wasn't what he looked like from the outside in, or even playing the part with convincing enthusiasm as he learned the business of the corporate world. The difficult part was when the voices started boiling over in his head... after he had convinced himself that things *really were* ok. He'd actually bought into the whole sales game and was becoming very successful at it. The recognition of his top sales performance from everyone in the company had fed a part of him in a way that he hadn't experienced since his high school athletic victories. They were *seeing* him, praising him, recognizing him as *somebody.*

Somehow, along the way in his accelerated corporate success track, he had managed to readjust his internal thinking and beliefs to match this outside world. It was as if he had been brain-washed and just quietly tucked his Bohemian side away. He adapted to the roles he was playing and *became* that person, because he knew the *real* him was just too 'out of the box' for the rest of them to handle. He dropped out of touch with his artist friends, isolated with Rachel and her socialite business acquaintances, and gradually acquiesced into this new lifestyle. Burning Man had become a thing of the past....

But inside he was slowly dying. It was only a matter of time before he felt a compelling need to somehow put his secret inner personal mark on the corporate world. It wasn't really a conscious or intentional effort. It was more like a hole inside of him that he somehow needed to fill. Adapting his behavior and thinking had worked well for a while, but eventually his resistance to this grew so great that he was forced to take another approach...trying to change the *outside* world so that it would match his *inner* thinking and beliefs instead.

So he began to push and probe just a little here and a little there. He would make suggestions that he thought would help humanize and equalize some of the inequities in the system that he perceived. He would make small comments at meetings that subtly questioned his boss. And therein lay "the rub", as Hamlet[3] had referred to it. He was quietly creating more and more conflict at work, in an unconscious attempt to make this hard reality of the external corporate world fit his internal personal belief system. He had done the best he could–without even realizing it–to bury his internal core values so that they wouldn't conflict with this external world. But enough was apparently enough, and his body and behavior were beginning to react to that unnatural shift. He had rationalized it over and over in his head:

After all, there are issues of fairness at stake...not just to me, but to my fellow workers. Why don't the others speak up? They all know there's politics behind some of these decisions. They know that some of these execs play golf together, chum around outside of

*work and who knows what else? Someone has
to speak up and make this right!*

How foolish he had been to think that he could single-handedly change the reality of that world! Yet being fired had really been a blessing in disguise. The real injustice wasn't the inequalities in the workplace and the apparent suffering created by that. The real suffering was his inner turmoil trying to make a round peg fit into a square hole!

Come to think of it, he didn't even want to categorize himself as a round peg! That would have been *their* description of him. No, he thought of himself more as an amoeba shape, constantly shifting and growing, and the world he had chosen to place himself in had spit him out for a reason…because it was not the right place for him to grow! Of course, he could see it all clearly looking back, but "hindsight is 20/20," as the saying went. Once it was over and he was officially out, all he needed to do (not that he knew it at the time) was disassociate from Rachel and stop trying to fit into *her* world as well. If he could manage that, then maybe he could be himself again….

Eventually–a few torturously long years later–he found himself free from her as well. He had settled into the basement of the converted church music studio and was pretty certain that he had finally arrived at a place of peace…a place where both his inside and outside worlds could align. If he could simply hole up in his studio and not have to deal with the outside world (except to venture out occasionally to sell some art), then perhaps all of his struggles manifesting as these constant inner voices in his head would finally go away....

Aaaah...if it were only that easy! In fact, when he finally found himself home alone with no corporate crap or Rachel to deal with, he learned the truth. All the voices, all the struggles and all of his suffering were still there, as loud and clear as ever! His self-talk and self-criticism, particularly around his painting, were screaming ever so much louder each day as he stood in front of his canvas.

Brink knew there must be another way to finally beat this conflicted way of living. How could he get his thinking and beliefs to somehow correspond to the world around him without all of this constant clashing? There must be some way other than bending his internal thinking or changing the external world itself, both of which seemed to be futile paths. Was it possible to create a more harmonious, less stressful way of being in the world ...perhaps even a *joyful* way?

He had studied Eastern philosophy and alternative schools of thinking back in school...he had even tried meditation for a while. The problem with that, of course, was that he had to *sit still*...which somehow just didn't appeal to him. No, he felt that he should be able to move around in the world on a daily basis interacting with people and situations without all of this second-guessing. He vowed to find a way out that would allow him to live his life without this ongoing torment! He would find a way, if it was the last thing he did....

tHe StRaiGht - 6

"You OK? Hey there...Mr. Brink, are you OK?" he heard the voice ask him again. Snapping to, he realized where he was...sitting in Olivia's kitchen.

"Yeah...sure, why do you ask?" he replied.

"Why do I *ask*?" she said, with a bit of disbelief in her voice. "Because you just suddenly kind of disappeared sitting there, staring off into space like that for so long, that's why." Then, in the kindest of voices she offered, "If you don't mind my sayin' so, I think you might have a bit of fever or something. Unless you're in some big hurry to get somewhere, I'm not so sure it's a good idea for you to be climbing back in that car of yours too quickly....By the way," she said, "that's a nice Falcon you're driving."

"Well, it used to be," he replied, putting his hand to his head to check for fever. "It was my Dad's. He died last year and left it to me. It really needs some work done on it, though."

"Sorry to hear that," Olivia replied.

"Oh, thanks. It's ok though," Brink said with a resigned tone. It's still drivable."

"No, silly!" she said shaking her head. "I meant sorry to hear about your dad."

"Oh, that's OK. He didn't really have a lot to keep him going… kind of drank the life out of himself, if you know what I mean," said Brink, letting out a sigh. "He did love that car though. It's a '67…one of the third generation Falcons… leather interior. A/C's not working right now and the driver's window and door won't open… but other than that it just keeps humming right along."

"I know!" she replied with vigor. "It's got that Ford straight-6 engine with the single-barrel carburetor…can't go wrong with that!"

Brink looked almost stunned. *How would she know that?* he thought to himself.

As if to be reading his mind Olivia continued, "I know, you're probably wondering how on earth I would know that. It's just that my Gramps drove one almost like it… well, actually it was a '63 Futura two door sedan… last of the *first* generation."

"Wow, you're kidding!" Brink exclaimed.

"Not at all…in fact, it's stored in the barn out back. I don't really have a need for a car very often, but it still runs fine. Body's in pretty good shape, too. I've only started it up a few times 'cause someone told me that was a good thing to do every once in a while if a car sets." She paused for a moment, as if quietly deliberating, then said, "We can take a look at it later if you'd like…that is, if you think you might stick around a bit. Where is it you're heading to anyway?"

"Oh, just this festival I go to every year…I'll tell you about it later. Hey, can I ask you just one more thing?"

"I guess you're getting warmed up now!" she said playfully. "What's that?"

"Why are you being so nice to a perfect stranger?"

"Well now, that's pretty simple, really," she declared. "You see, the other part that Grams taught me about being wary of people who ask for too much, was to always share all you can for those who never ask for anything. And I have to say, you haven't asked for a single thing from me, not even the glass of water I had to force feed you last night to get you to come to. You almost passed out you know! And if I do say so, you're not lookin' like you're quite up to snuff just yet either." She finished off by saying, "So seriously, you're welcome to stay another night on the couch out there if you need to. It's no big deal, really."

"I hadn't really thought about when exactly I was leaving, to be honest," said Brink. "I mean, I've been making pretty good time the last couple of days, but I don't really have a set deadline to get where I'm going."

Olivia laughed and broke into a smile.

"What's so funny?" he asked.

"Well, you sure are spending some time in that head of yours thinking about *something*, cause you don't seem like you've been *here* the whole time….No matter though," she continued, "C'mon with me. If you like my other painting so much, I'll show you what I've done in my studio."

She slipped out of the kitchen, back through the parlor and opened a door on the far side, with Brink and the cat following right behind. "This used to be my bedroom when Grams was still alive, but I use her old bedroom upstairs now. I really don't have a need for a guest room, so I just decided to use it for my art. Nice light in here, don't you think?"

Brink looked around in amazement. The room was filled with paintings of all sizes and shapes, colors and images. Some pencil drawings, water colors, oils, abstracts and landscapes. *How could this woman out here in the middle of nowhere learn to paint like this?* he marveled to himself.

"So...you did all of these, too?" he stammered ever so slightly.

"Pretty much," she shrugged. "I really don't have lots else to do out here. The town's pretty quiet except for the diner; that's about as exciting as it gets around Busy and I've got to do something to relax when I'm not working. The house really needs some more painting and fixing up, but that's more like doing chores really. I'll get to that one of these days."

"I don't mean to be rude," she continued, "but I've got to get back for the lunch shift. There's a few regular church goers who count on me for their Sunday meal. Let me just show you one more thing before I head back, though. She drew back the light curtains that had been in front of the double doors and opened the doors outward, practically skipping through them.

Brink followed her through the doors and, once again, his amazement continued....

~ 12 ~

The garden

Through the doors was a world that Brink would never have expected. Having driven through the relatively barren, dry plains for hours the day before, and then pulling into the dusty remnants of the town, he never in his life would have pictured what he saw in front of him at that moment. It was a garden…a garden so lush with greenery and life that it felt like it should be in a fairy tale book.

There were lots of desert-like plants, of course, including a variety of cactus plants with their characteristic hairy, thorny, thistle-filled look. Then there were the aloe vera types with their thick, juicy, shiny surfaces glistening in the sun. Scattered amidst those were small shrubs with downy, gray-green foliage that blossomed with purple, golden and multi-colored leafy flowers.

"These are pretty, and smell wonderful!" said Brink pointing at the bushes.

"Oh, those are all sage," Olivia replied. "Grams used it for everything in her cooking. She put it on salads and meat and poultry and loved to use it as the main herb for stuffing the turkey at Thanksgiving. She loved caring for her plants, but always had a practical side to her at the same time!" Brink scanned the garden, taking it in as Olivia continued to point out and name the variety of wildflowers.

"That tall one with the pretty yellow flowers is Agrimonia, not to be confused with the yellow Beggarticks over there. The pastel blue ones that look like a starfish are called Bellflowers. Then those other ones that have a similar starfish look are the Bur Cucumbers. They're one of my favorites; Sicyos Angulatus is the technical name. There's something about the way their flowers seem to float in mid-air that makes me almost feel like I am swimming underwater with them!" Olivia said, letting out a small squeal of delight.

There was no question in Brink's mind that somehow this garden fed a part of Olivia in an indescribable way. Although he didn't quite consciously understand why, Brink could feel a sense of peace in his body as he took the rest of the garden in....

Scattered among the gorgeous plants were seats, benches, sculptures, trellises and other items made of twisted metal, iron and various scrap materials. Somehow it all blended together into the most beautiful, warm and inviting tapestry that was–truly–an oasis in the middle of this barren land.

"But...how could all of this be so rich and healthy with everything so dry out here?" he asked her.

"Well, I can't exactly take credit for all of this...but I do my best to keep everything alive and growing," she replied. "You see, Gramps started this as just a little patch of something special for Grams a bunch of years ago. He was a welder, actually, and sort of an artist himself in his own way. He hated to waste anything and just loved to build with scrap materials that were lying around to create things that other people hadn't really come up with before."

"Sounds like a pretty creative guy," said Brink. "With grandparents like that, I can see where you got your painting skills from."

"Well, to be honest, I think most people would be pretty surprised at a lot of folks out in these parts. Sometimes people pass through and it feels like they think we're just a bunch of hillbillies or something out here. But the truth is that this is a pretty hard life in the plains, and people have to be…well…industrious to survive. So a lot of folks just sort of invent things they think would make it easier to live with." She paused, and then continued, "There's something about the big distance between people that inspires new possibilities. There's a certain kind of 'seeing'[4] that comes out of living in this big emptiness out here that you really have to experience for yourself, I think. In a way," she finished the thought off, "the *absence* of 'stuff' is necessary for other objects to rise up and be created."

Brink listened to Olivia's comments and found himself almost stunned by their depth. Her observations were simple yet somehow very profound. He looked at her with an almost shocked expression on his face.

Olivia suddenly let out a laugh and pointed to his face. "You look like your eyes are out on stalks," she said, cupping her hand over her mouth to hide a smile that was breaking out.

"Huh?" he puzzled back at her.

"You know…your eyes are popping out of your head! That look on your face is exactly what I've been trying to tell you about folks coming through here. They all pretty much think that we're simple minded folk out here. Well, we are…and then we're *not* at the same time."

"I'm sorry," Brink started to apologize. "I wasn't meaning to stare. It's just that what you said a moment ago reminded me of something I read back in college."

"What was that?" Olivia asked.

"Oh, it was just a bunch of philosophy…not very useful or practical stuff, really."

"I'd be willing to bet it was one of the Existentialists," she said, smiling in a curious way.

Now Brink was definitely thrown for a loop. First she had floored him with her paintings and now, out of the blue, she was speaking like anything *but* his picture of a naive waitress out in the middle of nowhere! "Why, yes, actually. It was <u>Being and Nothingness</u>, by Jean-Paul Sartre, if you must know."

"Yes, Mr. Brink…I am familiar with that work, although I haven't read the whole thing. There's a copy of it on my bookshelves upstairs. You see, my Grandpa was a very avid reader, one of those self educated people that never stopped devouring books once he got a handle on the English language. When you live out here, as I said, there is not a lot to do to relax when all the chores for the day are over. I inherited quite a collection from him, but I keep it all upstairs separate from my studio. I don't like to even think about being *in my head* when I'm painting. It can ruin my experience of the *feeling* process."

Brink literally had to sit down at that moment. His entire image of this simple waitress from the plains had just been shattered...no, that wasn't right either. It had been *expanded* almost instantaneously. Talk about a paradigm shift! He felt almost ashamed at catching himself in the act of pre-judging this woman. She was, without a doubt, a bit of an enigma to him.

"I don't think we best get into any more of that conversation," she said, "We'd better change the energy around here before you go dialing back up into that head of yours again!" she said. "Besides, I've got to be back at work pretty soon, so let me just tell you the rest of the story about the garden before I go...if you're interested in knowing, that is."

"Yes, of course," replied Brink almost apologetically. "Please...tell me the rest...."

~ 13 ~

tHe wEll

"Gramps hand dug a well back here years ago and then made that," she said, pointing upward. "It's kind of rough looking, but it's one of the best working windmills you'll probably ever see…pumps the water out of the well when it's windy and puts it up in that holding tank over there. Then he made this drip-like underground watering system that feeds all of this and keeps it growing. He read about them doing that over in the desert in Israel and figured he could do the same here. He's also got the roof runoff draining into that tank, so it pretty much takes care of all the water we need back here…if it's doled out in little bits at a time."

"Sounds like your Grandpa was an ingenious man," said Brink.

"He sure was!" replied Olivia. "Besides pulling the water up from the well, the tower also catches the lightning every once in a while during the flash storms that pass through here. Most people worry about tornadoes, but Gramps knew that as many or more people have been killed from lightning strikes around here as anything. The tower keeps the house from catching it and burning down instead. He lost the original old barn that was with this place when they first bought it. That's when he built the smaller one out back with the metal roof; it's grounded for lightning, too."

"Anyway," she continued, the main thing is that the pump does its job. This garden has been thriving for a long time. Mostly it's just plants that Grams and me gathered up here and there from the plains…but with the watering system in place here they've had a chance to grow a lot more than they could out there," she said, turning her head over her shoulder to look out over the rolling plains behind the barn.

Brink couldn't help but notice what a lovely neck Olivia had. *Where did that thought come from?* flashed through his mind, as she turned back to look at him. "To be honest, I'm surprised there's any water out here at all," he commented, as he thought to himself, *The only water I remember seeing are those springs by the side of the road in my dream.*

"Oh, but you *would* be surprised!" she exclaimed. "You know that expression *'Still waters run deep?'*" she asked him.

"Yes, I've heard that," he replied.

"Well, even though it's barren on the surface all around here, the Ogallala Aquifer runs under most of Nebraska.

"What's that?" asked Brink quizzically.

"It's kind of like an underground lake that runs under most of the Great Plains," Olivia went on to describe, "…sort of a giant underground sponge with buried layers of sand and gravel that are saturated with water. It's big enough to supply water to about a third of the irrigated crops that are grown in this country, but most people have never heard of it," she said, with just a bit of a twinkle in her eyes. "Just another one of those deep secrets that us plain folk out here keep to ourselves," she said with the smallest of smiles breaking from the corner of her lips.

Brink couldn't help but spend just an extra moment taking in Olivia's sweet lips. It was almost as if they had been lifted from a painting and gently caressed into the rest of her sweet face. They were perfectly formed in and of themselves. No need for lipstick or a drop of makeup to cover up any part of this woman's appearance. *What a total contrast to Rachel!* he thought to himself. There was just something so profoundly authentic about the simplicity of her features that to try to embellish or hide any of them with even a speck of unnatural material would be blasphemy.

"If you don't mind me sayin' so, you seem kind of...well… lost," Olivia said with a slightly hesitant tone.

"Oh, I'm sorry…" Brink replied. "I guess I was just…well, I was just thinking about something sort of simple and complicated at the same time."

"When I'm feeling that way I usually spend some time sitting here in the garden. If you're not in a hurry to get somewhere, you're welcome to sit here a bit while I'm on lunch shift. Jackamo will keep an eye on you, won't you good little man?" she winked, with her deep, now greenish, eyes.

"I'd kind of like to get some clean clothes out of my car," he stammered. "Maybe I'll walk you back to work, if that's OK?"

"Sure, that would be nice." She smiled and turned, walking back into the house....

~ 14 ~

ThE EmpOriUm

Brink honestly didn't remember one bit of walking to Olivia's house the night before. It was as if he had blanked out after the diner and the pie. *The pie!* He could remember that clear as day, for some reason. After walking her to the diner, he picked some clean clothes out of the bag in the back seat of his car, tossed them in a small backpack, slung it over his shoulder, then turned and gazed toward the direction they had just come from. The walk hadn't been very far, maybe half a mile. For some reason, he just didn't want to start the car and drive it back. He was suddenly feeling peaceful and walking felt right in that moment.

He got about fifty feet from the car, then suddenly turned around and headed back toward it, not quite certain what was pulling him back. He stared at the trunk, then popped it open, holding it up with one hand while he reached through the folded flaps of the box marked 'IMPORTANT' that he had salvaged from his father's possessions. His dad hadn't left him much of value when he died besides this car that they both loved, an old Winchester rifle and a bunch of dirty magazines. He found himself thinking sarcastically:

Thanks for leaving me your legacy, Dad. You could have at least left me a nice fat life insurance policy. No such luck there, I guess.

He glanced at the rifle lying next to the box for just a second, then reached into the box and pulled out a drawing of his from kindergarten, one of the stranger items that his father had kept, for some reason. *Not sure why he hung onto this, of all things,* he found himself thinking, as he unconsciously clutched the drawing in his hand, gently closed the lid, turned slowly and started walking toward Olivia's house.

He ambled his way back, taking in the little 'town'. Not much there, really. The diner sat sort of in the center of a scattering of other structures. He could see the old motel Olivia had mentioned down the street at one end and what looked like a grain mill or feed supply place down at the other. The motel looked like it didn't have more than four or five rooms at most; but then, this little town –if you wanted to call it that– wasn't exactly on a main drag.

Of course, everything but the diner was closed because it was Sunday. There was a small barber shop, a post office and then another little storefront that looked like…well, he wasn't quite sure what it was. He walked over and peered past the sign in the dusty window:

Emporium: Anything and Everything

Yup, the sign was pretty much on target as far as he could tell. It was the strangest collection of items that he had seen in one place that he could remember. There were tools, like any hardware store would have. But then there was kitchen and cooking stuff, some food items, a couple of saddles and a small section of books in the back corner, along with a smattering of antiques...or maybe those were actually up to date items for this neck of the woods, he thought to himself. Another small sign hung over the counter that read:

Broken? Leave it with us and
we'll do what we can for ya

It made sense, he supposed. I mean, how many people even lived around these parts? So, of course they had to combine resources a bit to be practical.

It seemed almost like these old buildings had somehow just gathered together in the middle of nowhere. Then further down, just a ways past the end of the cluster of buildings on the main street, he could see a small church building. Definitely one of the smallest churches he had ever come across. But then again, it didn't look like the population base had ever been that large, from what he could tell. There were a handful of people just starting to come out the door. He figured they were probably on their way to the diner, just as Olivia had promised.

He continued and turned back down the small street that led back toward Olivia's house. Although there were barely a dozen houses on the street, he noticed how much space there was between them. While it did resemble a street, it didn't feel anything like the neighborhoods he had ever lived in growing up. They all looked well-lived in and, overall, fairly well cared for. Porches seemed to be commonplace, and that feeling that the houses didn't crowd one another was very evident to him.

As he passed the last house, he noticed a bench just sitting off to the side, angled to the view down the road toward Olivia's house. It didn't seem connected to the last house at all; somehow it was just sitting, as if it naturally belonged there. There was no one around, so Brink decided to just sit for a few minutes and enjoy the view. Clearly someone had put it there for that very reason, so he was fairly certain that no one would take offense at him also stopping to enjoy it.

Olivia's house was not far from the edge of the little town, tucked off on its own, yet somehow still loosely connected to this cluster. As he sat there, Brink's mind flashed back to his dream, and once again he could almost feel the magic of swooping down from the clouds in the Falcon. Of course he knew that wasn't real, but in his mind's eye it was as if he could suddenly see the whole little town from above. He could even see himself sitting there on the bench at that very moment in time, with the drawing sitting by his side that he had placed there just a moment ago.

That's odd, he thought to himself…

> *There it is again…that part of me that is watching me while I'm sitting here….*

He remembered having a similar thought earlier–the one he had bookmarked as he had pulled into the diner the night before.

Each time he used the 'bookmarking' technique, he was reminded of his mom. This time, as he sat on the bench, his mind wandered back to his mom and dad when they were still together. They seemed so incredibly different to him, so he couldn't help but sometimes wonder how they had even ended up together. She had been brought up on a commune of sorts somewhere out in California…a community family living situation with the kid responsibilities, meals and other chores all shared by the adults living there. It wasn't an extreme arrangement like some of those with one husband and a bunch of wives. It was just a way for people to be close, help each other, and share resources.

His father was almost the polar opposite…a backwoods, gun carrying, rough around the edges guy from West Virginia. He made her laugh all the time, at least according to what she used to tell Brink. "He's just a stitch a minute," she had said on more than one occasion.

Well, that must have been a long time ago, thought Brink, because he sure didn't remember his father laughing much at all. Something had changed somewhere along the way, but for whatever reason his mom never did seem to come back to those bookmarked questions about his dad.

He thought about how nice it would be to see her again; it had been almost five years since she had flown out to visit with him and Rachel. His mom never hesitated to tell him how much she loved him. She had moved back to California to be closer to her aging folks a long time ago…as soon as he had grown-up enough to be on his own. He hadn't even talked to her in six months and doubted if she even knew that his dad had died. She hadn't even mentioned her ex in years; the hurt was so bad from his father having left them both.

But he had decided that he wasn't even going to tell her he was coming out that way. He really didn't want the pressure of a timetable on him. *Besides,* he thought to himself, staring at the drawing lying on the bench, *I really need that time at Burning Man to just chill out.* It had been way too many years since he had made it to the festival, which was probably why his creativity had been in such a slump. Being there–surrounded by so many explosively creative people–always seemed to give him a surge of energy that he desperately both craved and needed for continuing with his art. But somehow, no matter how good that surge was, the effect of it never seemed to last very long on him….

~ 15 ~

inSidE~oUt

Brink sat comfortably on the bench gazing once again down the road toward her little farmhouse in the distance. As he relaxed, his mind wandered back to Olivia. She was…well, quite different from any woman he had ever met. She most certainly was different from Rachel!

That's when it dawned on him that the whole time he had been sitting in the kitchen talking and listening to Olivia, *the voices had not been there*—with the exception of that one small instance when she had laughed as he asked his "first question." Except for that one moment, there was almost no second-guessing what she might be thinking of him, and in fact he really had no concern about what she *did* think about him. It had been just a very simple and present conversation about this and that…her grandmother and grandfather, the old cars, etc.

He had always had an eye for beautiful women, and Olivia certainly fell under that description…although he had finally reached the point of being comfortable with being alone and not actively looking for anyone. He did confess to himself, however, that the more he was around her, the more attracted he felt.

As he thought back on Rachel, as well as several of his other more significant relationships, he very clearly recalled that the voices were pretty much *always* there, plaguing him with self-doubt, especially during those initial encounters. *"Why would you ask a stupid question like that, Brink?"* he might say to himself. Or, *"I wish I wasn't dressed so sloppy right now. She looks so perfect; she'll never fall for me."* And, in fact, the voices and constant self-doubts stayed with him throughout his time with Rachel, right up to the end…like the instance when she had walked in and started questioning the quality of his artful jewelry pieces that day.

The more he thought about it, the clearer it became to him that every single time he had met an attractive woman, he had those self-doubts. It was as if he was just handing them over his power to hold over him in some way. But this time, with Olivia, there was something very different going on. It wasn't just his absence of feeling insecure, or possibly even being rejected. The voices simply were *not there*. It was similar to when he got 'in the zone' while painting. It didn't happen as much as it used to, but there were times that he literally had lost track of time and painted straight through the night, not ever struggling or being aware of the time passing…not ever once questioning or judging what he was creating.

The *flow* of being around her in this completely unselfconscious way seemed so easy; there was simply a naturally relaxed, very *present* communication with her. Yes, he had apparently spaced out somewhat thinking back on his past while he had been sitting there with her. But other than that—and the one instance when she had surprised him with her remark–the thoughts in his head had not been about wondering whether she might be judging him. For the moment, he was OK with the one imperfect slip of self-doubt. Life wasn't perfect. He was feeling a ray of hope beginning to shine….

Brink was also aware that it was a common tendency when meeting new people to become enamored with them, rather than focus on negative traits that turned more familiar with deeper acquaintance over time. But he was convinced that the freshness surrounding Olivia was not simply a matter of her being new to him. He tried to focus in on what it was that was so different about her. Take her painting, for example. She had never had any formal training, just some basic teaching from her grandmother. Yet almost all of her work was...well, *breathtaking* was really the best word to describe it...or perhaps even *mystical* in some way. What was her secret? Why was it that she could produce such masterpieces with so little effort? He remembered what she shared that her grandmother had said about art:

"Just spend twenty or thirty minutes most days and do something with your art. Stick to the basics, even if it means doing them over and over again until it seems a bit boring. Eventually it will become a part of you, just like walking. You simply will *stop thinking* about it and it will become a part of you. But do remember this: *if ever you find yourself trying too hard to create something, just walk away from it.* If you find that you are doing it because you 'should'…walk away! Just leave it be and don't return to it until you really *miss* it...until you find yourself truly *wanting* to do it. Always *listen with your heart*," her grandmother had told her. "Paint just as you live…with nothing but good intentions. If you do that, all the rest will follow."

"And never," Grandma Violet had added, "let the little voices in your head make you stop doing what your heart is telling you to do! Those little pesky critics inside your head are not YOU! Let the positive voices stay, and catch all the others and release them before they take you down with them.   Don't let the voices talk you in or out of doing your art... or anything else for that matter! It's OK to *notice the voices*, but in the end you must simply *follow your heart. It is the only thing you can always rely on to be the true you."*

Hmmm…that's strange, thought Brink. He knew he wasn't the only one on the planet with voices running through his head. But that last part her grandmother had thrown in about *noticing the voices.* That was exactly what he had remembered, and bookmarked, at the end of his drive last night. Apparently there was a way–at least according to Olivia's grandmother–to deal with those constant thoughts and voices rising up. And then there was the piece about *following your heart.* Somewhere in there was the secret to dealing with his inner turmoil, and he was bound and determined to figure it out….

His mind jumped back to Olivia and Rachel again, and he tried to pinpoint just what it was that was so different about the two of them. Rachel was almost the exact opposite in so many ways. She was a talker, and constantly self-consciously looking around to see what people would think of her. That was actually a bit of a mirror for him, reflecting his self-doubts around women. But Rachel was very extreme, constantly occupying herself with how she looked, what she should wear, and all that woman stuff. She was a looker; that was for sure. But she was a *put together* looker. It was as if she dressed, talked and acted in constant anticipation of what others would think looking at her...a sort of 'outside-in' approach to living.

Olivia–on the other hand–seemed totally relaxed and at ease with herself. She didn't use fancy make-up or have any apparent concern for looking a specific way. She just seemed comfortable–not to mention slim and sexy–in those well-worn jeans and her casual top. Unassuming was the word that popped into his head. And there was *no drama* in his interaction with her or, for that matter, anywhere that he could tell in her life...at least from what she had shared of it with him so far. Her parents had been killed and yet she had never said a word about 'poor me' the whole time she had talked about it. She didn't live in her past, as a victim of her circumstances; instead it seemed that she somehow chose to simply move on, being with and learning from her grandmother...almost as if her life had never skipped a beat from what must have been a traumatic experience losing both of her parents.

What was different about Olivia wasn't just in her dress and level of self-comfort, however. It was something about the *way* that she interacted with him that was not what he was typically used to experiencing. She was simply *there…present* in a profound way. She didn't seem to be trying to get any reaction out of him and certainly didn't appear to have a particular agenda. His conversations with her had just flowed naturally back and forth. Daydreaming aside, his usual barrage of thoughts that typically led to questioning himself had disappeared while he was engaged in conversation with her…a painless experience overall.

The best he could come to describe the difference between the two was that–while Rachel seemed to be put together from the 'outside-in'–Olivia was simply being herself from the 'inside-out.' *Very refreshing,* he thought to himself.

So, the real question was how–and why–was that the case? What was it that made Olivia's energy seemingly flow along in the moment…and was living like that something that Brink could get a handle on for himself?

~ 16 ~

eNerGy FlOw

Since he truly did not have an agenda at the moment, and since no one seemed to be around or concerned about him sitting on the bench at this informal little 'park', Brink continued to simply sit and follow his train of thought, observing where it went.

The question of what seemed like a magical energy flow in Olivia was not really a new topic for him. There had been a time a few years ago when Brink had found himself in a very stuck place with his art and creative energy. So he had decided to focus on learning more about people's energy flow in the hopes that it might improve his own. He began to consciously experiment with energy flow in his paintings and became consumed with watching people and trying to understand how the flow of energy around them showed up.

His favorite thing to do used to be to visit the airport and just watch all the activity, because it offered a good observation point for large variety of people all gathered in one place. And, it was different than going to a mall, where most people were generally more relaxed. He watched people of all shapes, sizes and ages moving about or just sitting in place. He knew others were also intrigued by watching people; but his level of involvement and intensity was almost consuming. He could spend hours at a time simply observing people and how their energy moved.

As he watched them, his mind filled with imagining the *thoughts* that must be going through their heads. He played with colors and other variations on his canvases to mirror and match the varying energies that he observed, resulting from his projections of their thoughts. There was extreme hurry, almost panic, in some cases. Then there were those not moving so fast but clutching and watching their possessions constantly. All of those, he judged, were the fear-based people of the world. *"Oh, my gosh! I can't miss my plane…I better keep a very tight hold on this bag so no one steals it…I hope my hair doesn't get messed up running for this darn plane!"*

His semi-abstract drawings and paintings exuded a variety of colors and wavelengths…some coming directly out of people's heads and manifesting as visual thoughts without letters. He judged that they, like him, were constantly bombarded with thought patterns over and over again. Their thought patterns reflected their fear, or a sense of adventure, or perhaps their love…like the mother and children that he found himself glued to observing one day.

Aha! thought Brink, a light bulb suddenly going off in his head. *A lot of these thoughts seemed to be tied to people's emotions.* On the surface this seemed obvious, but the fact was that thoughts and emotions were really two distinct types of things. One was a *thought* in one's head; the other was a *feeling* in one's body. He sensed, in his own body, that there was a need to make a deeper correlation between people's thought patterns and their emotions. Somehow, if he understood better what that correlation was, he might be able to make a breakthrough relating to their flow of energy. And, of course, that was the key he was looking for to *free himself* from being stuck in his own self-torturing patterns.

That's funny, he thought, sitting on the bench looking out, *Olivia mentioned something about keeping her books away from her studio so she wouldn't slip back into her head while painting. There is, for sure, more to that woman than meets the eye!*

Brink had reflected on this difference between thought and emotions, and recalled the various core emotions he had learned at a men's circle he had visited back in Atlanta. It seemed that most feelings really could be boiled down to five basic ones…anger, sadness, joy, fear and shame.[5] He began watching for these variations of feeling expressions in his observations of people, and resolved to study the energy flow of each emotion individually.

It dawned on Brink that–given the backdrop of the terrorist attacks on 9/11 and the increased security measures at airports–the atmosphere there was probably somewhat biased toward cultivating fear. He finally concluded that in order to get more of a scientific cross-section illustrating the other core emotional energy patterns, he would have to branch out to other locations.

So he had started visiting gymnasiums and fight training clubs to observe what he interpreted in many cases as anger. But then, he thought, all a person really had to do was go to a sporting event and wait for a referee to make an unpopular call and the anger from the crowds would well up naturally. Anger seemed almost as easy to observe and capture as fear. Those two emotions definitely seemed to dominate his observations up to that point.

Next he had started going to cemeteries to watch funerals and their associated outpourings of grief. One time he had gotten close enough to hear a bit of the ceremony and learned that the man had lost his wife and child in a car accident. Brink noticed how truly uncomfortable he himself felt as he had observed this man crying. It struck him that he had never before seen a grown man cry…certainly his father never had, at least not in front of him. He recalled just then that in addition to the advice his father had given him on playing sports and gaining a practical skill or trade of some kind, his father had told him to 'man up' and keep an eye on his mother. *"Real men don't cry,"* he had said to him in that moment when Brink's eyes had begun to tear up, realizing that his father was about to leave him for a long, long time.

Why hadn't Brink remembered that until just then? Why was it OK for the man at the cemetery to be crying? He certainly looked like a real man, and it certainly seemed very natural to see him grieve so deeply. As he thought more about it, Brink realized that, in fact, he had kept to his father's advice. He couldn't actually remember a single time that he had wept, let alone personally experience anything close to the grief of the man there to bury his wife and child. In fact, there had only been one instance as a child that he could remember crying even a little bit. He had fallen off his bike and torn his knee open pretty badly, and had cried just a little bit from the physical pain. But crying from a place of emotional pain? Not a chance….

The wash of sadness he had felt at the cemetery was more than Brink bargained for, so he had decided to take a break for the rest of the day. Next on his list was the search for observing joy, which he thought would nicely counterbalance the energy of grief or sadness. After that, and last on his list, would be the fifth and final core emotion of shame. He had thought about that one, and knew that shame would be a bit more challenging to capture…perhaps even elusive; so he had placed it as the last task on his project list.

Brink needed some groceries at home, so he had pulled into the local market to pick up a few things. When he hit the third aisle over, he suddenly came across a father scolding his son over something the young boy had done. Immediately he had observed the heaviness in the child's face, combined with the child's gaze moving down toward the floor. He knew that he had lucked out in coming across observing the emotion of shame in action[6].

What had followed immediately after the child's reaction, however, threw Brink a bit off balance. The father, having seen his son's reaction to his scolding, knelt down and looked the boy right in his eyes. He spoke something quietly to him, and then embraced him with a soft, loving hug. Brink had watched silently, suddenly feeling very uncomfortable inside. A wave of almost slight nausea came over him. He was so uncomfortable that he had to leave the store to get some fresh air. He tried to remember if perhaps he had eaten something earlier that might have given him a bit of indigestion; but underneath, he couldn't help but feel that there was something else....

~ 17 ~

JoY!/CoNnectIon

Between his observations and reaction to the man grieving at the cemetery and his experience of the father speaking with his son at the grocery store, Brink had felt incredibly drained. He decided not only to end his observations for that day, but to take a little time off before continuing his project any further.

Given that he had checked fear, anger, sadness and even shame off his list earlier than anticipated, only the feeling of joy remained left to explore. Logically, it seemed to Brink a great excuse to take a bit of time to really *feel* that…so he decided to take the full day's drive to Myrtle Beach, find joy at its peak, and just relax for a few days.

He was right, of course. All he had to do was arrive at the beach and he immediately had found all of the kids splashing around and playing in the sand. If that wasn't joy in its simplest and purest form, he couldn't imagine what a better example would be! It seemed very natural for children to hold the energy of Joy, and it was an easy task for him to visualize the bright and colorful transition of that energy onto his canvas. *But,* he wondered, *what about adults?*

As he lay there relaxing, Brink felt pretty good overall about his research up to that point. He had only to observe Joy in adults–mainly to satisfy his own curiosity– and he would be well on his way to laying the groundwork for his fabulous color-based canvas approach. Being the avid Facebook junkie that he was, he had been scanning places and events as he sipped on a cool drink, and had noticed a posting about a 'Laughter Yoga' meeting happening that evening nearby. He'd never heard of this before, so he made a mental note to check it out for himself later that evening. Then he rolled over, shut his eyes, and took a well-deserved nap in the sun....

As it turned out walking into the room that night, he knew immediately that this wasn't anything like traditional yoga. Apparently about 6000 groups around the world simply met to share pure laughter, and the reference to yoga in the Laughter Yoga[7] was related to the breathing and energy flow of the participants. There were no jokes told, just a variety of exercises that got the participants laughing to stretch their laughter muscles! One person would start with a "Ha!" and the next would repeat the first, then add something else, like "Ha Ha!"...then the third, "Ha Ha Hee!"...then "Ha Ha Hee Ho!" and so forth.

At first it seemed to Brink that the laughing was being forced a bit. But as the exercise progressed around the circle, people began to laugh as a natural response and soon it seemed that everyone in the room was laughing joyously, looking each other in the eyes, connecting, and truly having a wonderful time. The colors he saw blending in his mind in the energy exchange of the give and take of this laughter between the people blew his mind! Their energy was absolutely contagious and grew exponentially in just minutes.

A light bulb went on in Brink's mind as he observed the laughter participants. That was it…or at least a large piece of the puzzle! It wasn't just about the *one way* energy of fear turning inward, or about angry people sending their energy outward, or people like Rachel splattering her 'colors' on others. The key was somewhere in the processing and exchange of the energy *between* people.

Like his observations about the difference between *thoughts* and *emotions,* that might seem glaringly obvious on a certain level. But what Brink noted more than anything was that the laughter participants were happy, flowing and connected…and certainly as fully *present* as any of the people he had seen in various other states. It was as if they were *breathing in* the laughter of those around them, somehow processing it within themselves, and then responding by breathing out their own laughter. How refreshing! And–he surmised relative to his thought theory–they were so busy laughing that their minds had no room for all of their self-talk voices!

Yet try as he might to relax and get into it himself, Brink couldn't quite lose himself to the laughter as everyone else appeared to be doing. Something in him just felt sort of 'stuck.' And realistically he knew that even though the laughter seemed to reflect the right flow and response of energy, he couldn't just go around laughing to stop his barrage of thoughts…even if he *could* get into it. Yet somehow it was an analogy to the key that he had been searching for…a way to keep his energy flowing and interactive with the people and events surrounding him at any given moment.

Brink now had several key pieces of the puzzle of people's energy flow falling into place. There were the core *emotions* and the *thoughts* which resulted from those (or did the thoughts come first and then generate the emotions?). Then there was *the direction of the energy* to be considered, including the energy *exchange* itself…sometimes directed inward, sometimes outward, and sometimes seemingly more *connected* to those around than at other times.

And what all of this was really about, he reminded himself, was an attempt to solve the unending turmoil and suffering of his *own* thoughts and self-judgments, and the resulting negative emotions and energy patterns. He was tired of living his life trapped in this prison of thoughts with the constant bombardment from his inner critic second guessing him. That, coupled with his own fears, anger, shame and sadness, seemed to turn his life upside down on an almost daily basis.

All four of those emotions were simply way too ever-present in his life. Didn't he deserve more *joy* as an alternative? It was as if he was imprisoning himself in a cell with the never-ending negative outpourings of his thoughts, sparking the heaviest of the emotions on this roller-coaster ride called life. But weren't roller coaster rides supposed to be FUN?

Overall, he was encouraged by his observations of the energy flow patterns that he had captured, and felt mildly hopeful that he was finally on track to a solution for his years of self-punishment. Now that he had the backdrop of the emotional colors and energy flow ready to put on his proverbial canvas, Brink was ready to hone in on the real subject matter…the source and nature of the thoughts themselves.

If he were to stop the constant barrage of thinking–or at the very least get a handle on it–he would need to know much more about *what* thoughts were made of, *where* they came from and, certainly, *why* they continued to rise up in him. *What made me think…that I could, or couldn't, do something?* he thought to himself…

> *What made me think…that I should…or shouldn't? What made me think…at all?*

~ 18 ~

tHe DrAwiNg

Brink took a deep breath and gazed out over the plains in the distance again. Then he looked down at the picture lying on the bench next to him. He had no idea why he had gone back to the car to take that drawing out of the box in the trunk….

Why didn't I just burn this silly picture with the rest of my dad's stuff? What's so important about it anyway? Talk about a good example of what makes someone think anything at all…I didn't even actually think about taking this picture out of the trunk. I just sort of did it without thinking about it. What's up with that?

But he just kept staring at it, almost paralyzed…or was the drawing staring at *him?* He shifted on the bench a bit and then picked up the drawing to study it more closely. It was a fairly simple picture of a meadow, showing some rolling hills with flowers in the foreground, a few scattered trees and–as is common in so many young children's drawings–the sun shining down on all of it. In the foreground was a young boy–probably him–sitting on a big rock. There was a butterfly perched on the boy's knee.

Looking at it now, it really didn't seem like anything special; he couldn't even remember creating it. Honestly, it looked like most young children's first attempts at primitive art. Yet his dad must have liked it; otherwise he wouldn't have kept it all these years. And the message written at the bottom definitely was not characteristic of his father. There in the lower corner, was scrawled in ink:

I love you son.

Dad

That's strange, thought Brink to himself, *I never really noticed that before…or have I?*

Yet somehow that picture was actually what had started this whole trip. He'd been cleaning out his dad's house with his friend Damien. They had taken a truckload of things to the Salvation Army, thrown a whole bunch of other stuff out, and then burned what they could in the fire pit in the backyard. He was poking through this box of stuff marked *"IMPORTANT"* …which was, of course, mostly more crap that his dad wouldn't let go of. He was sorting through the box tossing things into the fire, taking the time just to make sure he didn't overlook anything that might *actually* be important. So what was so significant about that stupid little drawing?

He recalled the moment that he had discovered it sorting through his dad's possessions. He had stared at it then just as he was staring at it now. That message at the bottom… apparently he *had* seen it before. The thing of it was that his father had never actually told him directly that he loved him as far as he could ever remember. Likewise, it wasn't as if he had expressed anything like that to his dad either.

"Hey man…hey man, are you okay?" he recalled Damien calling over to him as he had stared at the picture, frozen in time. He had looked up without saying a word. "You look like a deer in the headlights, Bro," he could hear Damien saying again. 'Bro' was their word for brother, even though they weren't actually related.

"What's the matter with you anyway? You've been dragging your ass around for months, and now you can't even talk. I'm worried about you, Bro. I think you've got some serious issues going on. You're so lost in your head that I haven't had even a half decent conversation with you in weeks. Maybe you should go see a shrink or something."

Brink stared back at his friend…speechless.

"Seriously, now that your dad is gone, what are you sticking around this town for anyway? Maybe you should just go on a trip or something. Clear your head out…you know what I mean?" Damien had said to him.

"Yeah, that might be good," he had finally responded, taking in the idea. In that moment he had made the decision to pack it all up and head west, check out Burning Man and see his mother again to give her the news in person about his father dying. His vision was to head west with the intention of clearing his head of *all* of it...the memories of his father–both good and not so good–Rachel, his other past lives and most of all those plaguing negative voices in his head! He knew on some level that until those voices subsided, he really wouldn't be able to push further into his art, his creative self or whatever awaited him in the next chapter of his life.

So he had put a few of his cherished worldly possessions in the old Falcon...a couple favorite pieces of his own art, a duffle bag full of his clothes and a banjo that he hadn't picked up in about ten years. Although he didn't actually ever play it, there was something so very real about that instrument, and it comforted him in an unexplainable way to have it nearby. An old friend of his who lived out in the Ozarks had hand-crafted it, and it had taken him almost a year to pay for it. Whether or not he ever actually played it didn't even seem to matter.

The rest of his stuff–including his tattered furniture and all his art supplies–he had just given away. He was gone within a couple of days...and now here he sat, in the middle of Nebraska on a bench in some little town. Sure, he was physically in a different place...but did that really matter?

What am I going to do with myself now? I can run all I want, but is anything ever really going to change? The voices are still with me. I still have no idea what to do, what I want, where to go, really...am I ever going to get out of this mess? Maybe I should just walk back and trade this drawing in for that rifle in my trunk.

He stared at the drawing one last time, then folded it up carefully, and put it in his back pocket. He sighed deeply for a moment, thinking resignedly,

Well it is what it is. At least I can keep this as evidence that my dad did love me, I suppose.

He stood up and looked back up the little street toward his car for just an instant, shook his head silently, then headed down the road toward Olivia's house....

tHouGht pUZZLe

As Brink started to walk, a butterfly appeared dancing in front of him, as if to lead him down the path, making sure he didn't turn around to trade the drawing in for his rifle. Brink meandered along with his brain, as always, filled with thoughts.

His mind wandered back to the buzzing and energy that had filled every bit of the air at the airport. *Just how many thoughts went through each person's head in a minute, an hour, a day or even in a lifetime? Would it feel different–would it even be possible–to have a room full of people without thoughts for even just an instant?* He wondered to himself if he could ever have a day–or even just one hour–without thoughts constantly arising in him. Even the very thought of all of those thoughts was mind boggling to him!

> *Where did thoughts actually generate from? Could they be seen or measured scientifically in some way? Were they made of the same 'stuff' or 'matter' that the rest of the universe seemed to be made of?*

Like a good existentialist, Brink decided that focusing on the origin of thoughts themselves was not the real question at hand. To answer that would be like trying to answer the question of how humans got here, whether or not there was a Creator or Supreme Being versus the theory of Natural Evolution. The question of why we were given 'thoughts' and the multitude of tangents such a discussion would bring was definitely too much to take on!

No, the place to best start would be simply to accept the *fact*[8] that we humans simply *have* thoughts…and move on from there. So instead Brink decided to focus on the question, "What *purpose* do thoughts serve?" And, was it really beneficial for people–for *him*–to be thinking all the time?

He began by analyzing and categorizing different types of thoughts, and looking at their value in terms of the various emotions that he had been observing. There were *memories*, for example. For the most part many of those were quite enjoyable. And, of course, there were also those that were very painful. It occurred to him that in a certain way the good memories were just as uncomfortable as the painful ones. After all, the feeling of loss in *not having* or *longing* for those good times pictured in the memories was actually a form of discomfort and pain in itself.

Brink then moved from the general category of *past* thoughts and memories to *future-based* thoughts… illustrated by the fear of those folks running for their connection at the airport, or perhaps having their bag stolen. *I mean really,* he thought to himself, *did the energy of all of that anxiety actually serve them in some way? And while some might relish in the prospect of future positive possibilities, weren't those also a waste of energy in a certain sense?* It just seemed to him that the great majority of thoughts both past and future were not really serving useful, practical functions…certainly not in his own life.

So he turned to examining the nature of *present-based* thoughts, which seemed important since even the thoughts that we have about the past or the future occur *now*—in the present moment—not actually in the past and future. For some reason, the examples that jumped out for him from his own past thinking seemed mainly to involve other people. Thoughts such as *"What would they really think of me if they knew that?...I wonder if she likes my hair parted this way. Oh, my gosh…that last thing that came out of my mouth sure sounded stupid! Man, I'd like to get in bed with her!"* All of those also seemed to him, upon reflection, not to really serve any useful function except to feed internal anxiety or preoccupation of some kind.

One thing he did notice was that most of these thoughts seemed to fall into a general descriptive category of being *negative* in their nature. He'd certainly heard of "positive affirmations" to counter all of that negativity…the nothing-but-positive statements that all of the 'do-good' authors—as his inner cynic liked to call them—were always promoting. Well, maybe those at least had the potential as thoughts to serve some useful function, but the jury was still out on that topic for him.

So he left that tangent alone for the time being and returned to his observations about the functionality of present-based thinking.

Aside from the possible good influence of the positive affirmations that he was willing to entertain, there were *some* other present-based thoughts that seemed, at least on the surface, to serve some function. For example, *"Which exit number should I be watching for?"* or, *"That guy seems a little drunk and angry. I think I'll stay clear of him."*

So at least in some instances there appeared to be a practical aspect to some of the thoughts that filled people's minds. But by and large it definitely seemed to him that the storm of ever-present value-based *judgmental* thoughts was basically lacking in purpose.

Why am I even spending so much of my own thought energy thinking about all these thoughts? he actually found himself thinking. *And isn't it odd that in some way I am noticing and watching myself having all of these actual thoughts?* The bookmarked thought…there it was again! Each time it rose up and caught his attention, it baffled him. Yet in all of the elaborate delineation that he had laid out, this element of noticing and watching somehow didn't seem to fit into any of those thought categories.

Lurking beneath the surface, Brink could tell an undercurrent that was not to be ignored. Olivia's painting, the Dark Carobola, loomed in his mind's eye once again….

~ 20 ~

The Illusionist

Brink continued down the dirt road head toward the house, the butterfly still leading him along, dancing from side to side, as if to say, *"Take your time…relax and enjoy your walk and this beautiful day!"* So he continued to relax, pausing here and there for a few moments and gazing off, as he focused once again on the 'thought puzzle,' as he liked to refer to it.

There were so many paths that his brain could go down–analyzing the various categories and aspects of thoughts–that it was mind boggling. Brink knew there was a danger in going 'down the rabbit hole', and that he would have to take a step back in order to keep the big picture in focus. If he didn't stick to the basics, he would never make any progress with this huge task of reigning in his own thinking.

So he returned to the question of what the relationship was between the three major elements…the *thoughts*, the *emotions* and the *energy flow* of how they tied together. Like any good work of art, Brink knew that a solid grasp of all of this would more than likely not fit neatly into a box. There was always some deeper more intuitive understanding that came into play, at least where significant growth of any kind was at stake. And, the stakes here were big; this was his *life* he was trying to get a grip on…his own sanity and happiness!

Setting the variable of emotions aside for the moment, he now had a basic schema of the various *types* and *tenses* of thoughts to place against the backdrop of general energy flow. How was it that each person *interacted with their environment* within their thoughts? What was the *flow of energy* for each of those people? What different reactions with what different thought patterns did people have in the same situation?

His mind wandered back to a party he had gone to with Rachel one night. His radar scanned the room beginning with her as they entered. He hated to admit it, but now that he had experienced Olivia in her natural and completely unassuming way, he clearly saw that Rachel was indeed a prime example of one of those 'outside-in' people. She was incessantly consumed with how she looked to others, starting from the moment she spent getting ready to leave. Undoubtedly her pre-occupation had originated even long before that in her weeks of preparation for just going to the damn party, he speculated. On her way to making her grand entrance, he knew that her mind was absolutely filled with thoughts such as *"Who would be there? What would they think of her?"* and *"Would she look fabulous to them?"* In reality this wasn't just speculation because she couldn't stop asking those very questions out loud to him on the drive there!

As with everything, there were varying degrees of 'outside-in' and 'inside-out' people in Brink's schemata. For example, directly opposed to the self-conscious Rachel was the example of a drunk and disorderly person who really didn't care at all what anybody thought about him.

"What do you mean I can't have another drink?" he heard the already drunken guest stammer at the waiter hired to serve at the party. "You're just an overly concerned employee paid to serve the guests; you're not a bartender at a public place. I'll damn drink and do what I feel like until the party host tells me otherwise, so just do your job and don't worry about me staggering around!"

In a certain twisted way that person was freer than most, simply because his thought patterns and level of self-consciousness around others was brought to a basic level of dealing with the present moment only. At least, that was Brink's personal experience after he consumed an unfavorable amount of alcohol. But, as extreme as this example was in Brink's mind, it did illustrate the effect of people acting without self-consciousness about what others would think.

A more typical form of the 'inside out' person–and by far a more positive example than the drunken guest–was the person whom he judged was more naturally not ruled by what others thought. Such a person was simply comfortable with himself and did not waste a lot of energy worrying about the opinions of those around them. That is not to say that they didn't care what others thought; it seemed more as if they didn't use other's judgments as a guide for their behavior. For people like this, their energy appeared to flow more *from the inside out*, as was the case with Olivia.

There were a few examples of people like this who came to Brink's mind…people who seemed to genuinely reflect a certain calm and energy. For example, there was Mrs. Bellamy, one of his neighbors, who was an avid gardener. She always wore the same comfortable clothes while working in her garden, and seemed very present and peaceful. Sometimes he would exchange a few words with her when he would pass by on his occasional walks. He had learned that she had lost her husband almost a decade ago, and gardening seemed to be one of the ways that she would center herself. She even shared with him that her husband used to be an avid gardener himself, so in some ways she said it made her feel like she was with him again.

Brink thought about his favorite flannel shirt–full of holes and peppered with paint–which he loved to wear whenever he was at the canvas with his brushes. No one was watching him; he simply felt comfortable in it, feeling in his element… "comfortable in his own skin," he recalled the expression being. These were small moments of truly living from the inside-out without any self-consciousness of what others might think or judge. But sadly, those moments seemed few and far between.

As Brink stood on the dirt road staring into space and thinking about those simple moments, the butterfly once again landed, this time on his shoulder. It was as if it was trying to bring him back from getting too lost in his thoughts…to wake him up in some playful way and say, *"I said to relax and take your time, but don't miss this beautiful day all around you by getting lost in your head!"*

Yet Brink simply couldn't leave this puzzle alone. It was not so much the extremes that fascinated him, so much as those who seemed to represent the subtle variations on the core 'outside-in' and 'inside-out' patterns. His attention locked in on those people whom he judged to be incredibly sophisticated at creating the perfect *appearance* of living from the inside-out. They did not display their nervousness in the same outward way that Rachel did. No, they buried it really, really well….

The story Brink told himself was that some of them had been refining this sophisticated inside-out look for quite a long time. Yes, they had mastered this mask of the perfect inside-out appearance, and he hypothesized that there was no way they would let anyone see their true nature deep down. Of course, Brink knew that most of these theories were based on his own personal projections and imagination. He had no real documented evidence to support these energy or thought flow scenarios.

In a lot of ways the *visual* cues were the easiest to pick up on with regard to energy flow. How people dressed was of course an evident variable. The obvious ones were those like Rachel who were consumed with how they looked to others. Then there was the grunge crowd and the punkers who didn't *appear* to care at all what they looked like to others. And yet they did…because there was an art and style to non-conforming which Brink judged was really just a reactive expression to the masses. In their own way, weren't they equally as conforming as all of those conservatives?

It was mainly because of all of those subtle variations in appearance–and *apparent* appearance–that Brink knew he needed to have more than just visual evidence if he were to figure out this energy flow element. So he began adding more dimensions to his analysis, moving beyond just the visual to deeper *listening* patterns. After all, words and conversations were the manifestation of thoughts themselves. He was well aware of this own thoughts, but if he wasn't able to read people's minds, the only choice he really had was to track their words and conversations.

He didn't spend much time on the obvious ones like Rachel who consistently just wanted to babble on about themselves. Rachel was an easy subject to categorize; she was busy splashing her particular color of thought all over those around her. When she showed up at a gathering, he saw bright lime green, like the color roadside workers wear, splashed all over everyone near her...as if to scream, *"Look at me! Don't you dare miss seeing me!"*

It was the less obvious, more sophisticated inside-out people that intrigued Brink. On the surface they *appeared* interested in those they were engaged with....just as on the surface they appeared not to be concerned about how they looked. The classic example was a local college professor who showed up at the party wearing his well-worn favorite camel hair jacket adorned by the elbow patch on a single sleeve. It was as if to say *"I don't really care what you think. This is my favorite jacket and I am going to continue wearing it, patch or not."* Actually, that was quite believable...until he honed in on the perfect placement and stitching of that seemingly arbitrary patch. But again this was still a theoretical, not evidence-based, approach. What really gave his theory validity was the pattern of the verbal *conversational* flow as a means of looking more deeply at the true energetic pattern that lay underneath.

While the sophisticated professor did *appear* genuinely interested in asking questions of others, Brink observed that he would always bring the conversation back into his own domain...similar to a great magician or illusionist who redirects attention elsewhere in order to manifest something in a completely different place. The conversation ultimately came back to something that the professor could espouse on in order to illustrate his expertise...a means to his own end. It was a much subtler way than Rachel's overt way of demanding the attention of others.

In the end, Brink concluded, this type was essentially just another form of 'black hole.' It simply was not an authentic dialogue of two different energies mixing together and creating something greater than the sum of its parts. That is, the *apparent 'inside-out' un*self-conscious professor model led to the same results as the blatant extremely self-conscious Rachel model. The Professor, in this case, *was* concerned with how he appeared to others, but was simply a master of manipulation…just like the classic illusionist. Instead of screaming "Look at me!" he masterfully and subtly manipulated the conversation until it invariably and magically returned the focus of attention back upon himself.

There was something about this covert pattern that was just as unnatural as the overt form that Rachel's took. The pre-occupation with what others thought, and the energy that it took to craft the 'outside-in' appearance were somehow not *real*. Beyond that, it seemed to Brink that all of that pre-occupation and manipulation was an inordinate *waste of energy*. To be consumed with living one's life in constant reaction to others was not the way that he wanted to live!

Brink noticed how his theories observing others were really loaded with judgments about them. He didn't *like* the way Rachel and the professor were being in the world. Perhaps it worked for them, but that way of living would not work for him. Yet he had spent an inordinate amount of time so far in his life surrounding himself with those types of people! *What made me think…that living like that was what I wanted?* he wondered to himself….

~ 21 ~

TOWER OF bABbLe

The butterfly suddenly was dancing all around Brink's face, almost pestering him to awaken from his day-dreaming. Brink had no idea how long he had been walking; his sense of real time was pretty much non-existent at that point. It seemed like hours had passed as his mind had wandered back and rehashed those topics that he had returned to so many times before. It all seemed so terribly futile sometimes. *I'm just cursed,* he concluded.

> *There's no way I'm going to solve this thought puzzle. Maybe I should just rename it the "Thought Maze" and accept the fact that I will be lost in this labyrinth forever!*

The butterfly was still flitting around, but this time moving further away from him, dancing into the distance and disappearing, as if to say, *"I have delivered you safely, and now I must be off!"* He was now just a stone's throw from Olivia's house. As he approached the house, he realized that he was actually seeing it consciously for the very first time. He had zero recollection of getting there the evening before, and had not paid much attention to its details as he and Olivia had walked away from the house to the diner. Now, as the gap closed approaching it, he literally stopped in his tracks to take it all in.

The house itself was not in the best of condition on its exterior. It definitely needed a good scraping and painting; he had noticed that just from looking around the porch earlier when he woke up. The crying out for paint aside, it was a solid structure, with good clean lines. Not very big, really…a one and a half story with the porch larger than typical, but definitely creating a warm and welcoming addition. He imagined that the second floor probably didn't contain much more than just the bedroom that Olivia mentioned used to belong to her grandparents.

What struck Brink was the *setting* of the house itself. The backdrop included the small barn with its metal roof and the barren yet slightly rolling prairie that lay beyond. Although it was just a brief distance from the town center to here, the house seemed to be somehow perched on the edge of a vast open space that felt like miles from any civilization.

As he looked past the structures, he saw the wide open rolling prairie; it was dry, yet somehow alive, with almost knee-high grasses carrying the breeze along. There were some cattle grazing in the distance, but no apparent fences containing them. The land rolled a bit and didn't have any trees, except for what appeared to be one scraggly growth out beyond the cattle that might give them a bit of shade at times.

As simple as it was, and as empty as it was, the landscape somehow displayed a richness of its own. Although he passed through hundreds of miles of the Great Plains yesterday, the subtleties of color were not evident to him earlier. Yet in this moment he was seeing a depth that–for whatever reason–he was suddenly appreciating and registering in his consciousness.

Brink had never noticed how many tones of brown really existed. Brown had never been a favorite color of his. In his judgment, brown had no life of its own. It had always seemed to him just a boring filler against which he could set other objects in the foreground. Now he was seeing the wheat-colored light brown grasses against the brown earth and the scattered bushes. There were hints of green, but the entire landscape looked to him like a sepia photograph. The light of the day cast a soft glow over the land, which all blended together into one flowingly simple, yet scenic, eternal view.

He imagined the pioneers travelling across these lands and could feel the weariness that some must have experienced along the way, choosing to settle down at a certain point rather than continue to push forward. He could see Olivia's grandfather standing by the barn looking out on the land, and could almost feel the gratitude and peace of calling this place home. Something inside of Brink rose up, as if a slow breath of air were filling him from the ground up...and he let out a long, almost comforting sigh. One day maybe he would be able to settle in and appreciate the simplicity of the ordinary, rather than chasing after whatever it was that constantly drove him to look for something *more* in his life.

He refocused his gaze back toward the house and couldn't help but observe the windmill hovering over the roofline. It was the first time, at least that he could remember, that he was approaching the house from a distance. The tower was definitely a little odd looking and definitely not your traditional looking windmill. In fact, it was downright unattractive in his opinion! He remembered Olivia telling him that it was made from scrap iron and a collection of other materials that her grandfather Tomas had put together…all for the purpose of nourishing that beautiful garden.

Clearly, thought Brink laughing quietly to himself, *her grandfather had no concern whatsoever for anyone else's opinion of the aesthetics of this structure.* Brink intuited from this instance alone that her grandfather must have been a man of his own making….an 'inside-out' man who truly didn't act out of concern for what others might think of him or his creations. *Unusual, yet admirable,* Brink concluded, his mind glancing off years of self-conscious struggle with his own art creations. He stared at the tall, unattractive tower and his face lit up just a bit. *Why…if it isn't the Tower of Babble!* he thought, as he smiled inwardly.

He found himself thinking back to the time he had spent in a Philosophy PhD program at Northwestern. He had gone there because he was as fascinated with philosophy as he had been with psychology when he was in college. But after a year he became disillusioned…it seemed to him not unlike the Tower of Babel (or Babble, as he preferred to think of it). Each of the many PhD students and professors that were there, studying their various disciplines, seemed to be speaking their own language.

They each had a specialty, a theory or a thesis that they were devoted to; yet in order to espouse the wisdom of their particular frame of reference, they needed to draw you into their own particular vocabulary. So debates between any two parties were almost ridiculous, because more often than not they were speaking their own distinct language. There were just too many PhD candidates in the same place having to be right at the same time! And, to top it all off, those studying Phenomenology and Existentialism, like himself, were so young that they really didn't have much real life experience to which they could attach their theories. *Yeah, that really makes a lot of sense…so much for basing the meaning of life on anything concrete,* he remembered thinking sarcastically. But now, staring up at the tower, a smile came to Brink's face as he thought:

At this point, I think I'd take this ugly old tower over the Tower of Babble any time!

At least he could be proud of one thing…unlike the corporate gig where he had set up undercurrents to un-consciously sabotage himself, he had made a *conscious* decision to walk away from graduate school. Yet the voices had plagued him back then, too.

> *Is this the right place for me to be right now? How did I get here? What, or who, is really driving my bus? Am I doing the right thing walking away?*

Even back then, it had been almost impossible for him to get a handle on those internal voices and the constant self-doubt running through his mind. Being in school and learning itself was great; nothing wrong with that, of course. He had thought that studying psychology and philosophy might actually help him stop questioning himself. But instead it had the opposite effect. The questions compounded and the voices grew louder and stronger, multiplying as time passed. Now they were even more sophisticated on multiple levels. It was no longer just a question of "*Am I good enough?*" Now he was torturing himself over *why* he, like all the rest of the beings on this spinning planet, was even here at all!

So he had to take a politically correct 'leave of absence' from the program in the hopes that he could stop some of the constant thinking and quiet his mind for a while. But even though he had internally debated until he felt positive about the decision to drop out, as soon as he actually did it, the voices of self-doubt immediately rose up again....

*You had to quit this, too, huh? Can't you
stick with anything? You are such a loser!*

The boiling over of his thought processes began to
settle down a bit once he got out of that grad school
Tower of Babble. The more he stepped back from it, the
clearer he could see how people in each of the various
disciplines seemed to be constantly trying to impress one
another using their own unique descriptive terminology
as their personal armor. But no one was really willing to
let go of their personal opinions or attachments to really
hear someone else's side or perspective. Something about
it in his gut just seemed really unhealthy to be around.
Once he got enough distance from that academic
environment, he knew he would never go back.

Yet despite his growing comfort with the decision to
leave—and his inner critic settling down to just a simmer—
the voices never completely subsided. In his head,
'Quitter' was all he could hear his father saying *not* to
become, even though his father wasn't in touch with him
back then. Now that his dad had passed on and he had
gotten his small estate in order, maybe he could bury
some of those voices with him…or so he hoped.

Brink gazed past the tower to the barn behind it, and
the empty land beyond that….

*Will my thoughts ever stop running? Will I
ever be able to cut myself a break from all
of this self-criticism? It is torture living*

like this! Why can't my mind just be still and peaceful like this beautiful prairie?

The barn was a nice complement to the house. It was a story and a half tall, not quite reaching the same height as the house, but clearly providing useful functionality for this little homestead. It had a slight little lean to it, but seemed to be holding its own. Its rich burgundy-colored metal roof had a little rust in places, but it appeared to be solid and serving its purpose of keeping whatever was inside dry and protected.

Brink shifted his casual inspection of the property back toward the house with its screened porch, and his body's memory could feel the comfort of deep sleep that had enveloped him the night before. He suddenly felt exhausted, even though he was aware that he had slept late into the morning. He felt his own energy drained from reviewing all of his research on people's thoughts, emotions and energy patterns. It was all so damn complicated! Why couldn't it be as simple as the landscape he was looking at right now, rather than a barrage of complex systems and patterns that he just couldn't make any sense out of?

He was overwhelmed with all of it, and his body was screaming for sleep. Despite the fact that he must have slept at least ten hours the night before, that wicker couch was calling to him again! He looked up and there in the doorway was the orange cat, just sitting there, quietly waiting. He resisted the couch's invitation and decided instead to just sit on one of the wicker chairs and close his eyes to rest for just a few minutes. *There may just be something to this sitting still thing,* he thought to himself, as he sat down quietly for the second time since he had dropped Olivia at the diner....

~ 22 ~

ROuLeTTe

As Brink once again let his mind wander–this time behind the safety of his eyelids–he could see himself sitting...not in the chair on Olivia's porch, but rather in the seat of a small theatre of some kind. There, on the stage, was the Professor in his camel hair jacket. He had a white baton in his hand and was standing looking over a small group of people scattered about in front of him in no apparent order. It was as if he was a conductor, but there was no orchestra and no instruments.

The Professor stepped down from the podium and began to walk amongst the people. They were coming into focus for Brink now...many of them recognizable. Olivia was there; his eyes naturally were drawn to her before any of the others. She was standing behind a section of the diner counter, holding a plate of that apple pie in her hands. Nearby he could see a small cluster of people; and in the middle of them was Rachel, animated and talking as always. There was an older couple sitting in a pair of rocking chairs that didn't look familiar to him, but as he stared at them he somehow knew that they were Violet and Tomas, Olivia's grandparents.

Brink got out of his seat and walked closer, actually climbing the stairs to get a better look at the cast of characters. He saw his old boss from Corporate, and then his neighbor kneeling in her garden working quietly. Jackamo the cat was there, rubbing the back of his head against the edge of a chair leg. Off to the side were the people from the airport, clutching their bags for dear life. Finally, Brink's gaze fell on his mother contentedly reading in a comfortable chair by a fireplace.

The Professor began to walk around amidst the various people. One at a time, he stopped in front of each of the characters and–Tap.Tap.Tap.–touched his baton to their heads ever so gently. First to go were the fearful airport folks. As the Professor tapped their foreheads, their entire faces and bodies began to suddenly sprout thousands of small cracks…just like the face of the raku pot that held the delicious coffee Olivia had left for him. As the cracks spread rapidly from head to toe on each and finally reached the ground, Poof! The entire person simply collapsed into a pile of nothingness and disappeared!

The Professor glanced casually toward the audience, as if to check that they were paying attention, and then continued his walk around, moving next to Brink's old boss…Tap.Tap.Tap. Poof! Shattered and gone, just like that. Finally, the Professor moved over to Rachel and the small group gathered around listening to her… Tap.Tap.Tap. Poof! Not only did Rachel shatter and drop into a pile of nothingness, so did those around her, all at once! The Professor turned to the crowd seated in the theatre and nodded just a bit more at each of his own amazing disappearing feats.

Then he walked over to Brink's mother, still absorbed in her reading. Tap.Tap.Tap. Nothing. His mother remained just as she had been. Rather than press his luck, the Professor gently smiled as if to say, *"No problem; that was my intention."* He proceeded to Olivia's grandparents…Tap.Tap.Tap. Nothing. They remained. He moved on to Olivia with the same result…nothing. Finally, the Professor actually went over to Jackamo, reached down to gently scratch behind his ears, then let out a small sigh as he tapped on the cat's forehead. But, to the Professor's dismay, the cat remained as before, even a bit more content because his ears had been scratched.

The Professor turned to the crowd and stepped to center stage, unwilling to be seen as a failure. It wasn't clear to him what had gone wrong, but there was no way that he could leave things as they were. So he stood, looking out at the crowd, as if to say, *"I am not finished here, you fools!"* Then he raised his baton to his own head…Tap.Tap.Tap. A small crack appeared in the center of his forehead and slowly spread down and across his face, then continued on to his neck and shoulders…until his entire body had thousands of cracks running through it and Poof! The entirety of him shattered and dropped into a pile of nothingness and he was gone.

Brink looked around at the remaining cast of characters. Olivia and her grandparents and Jackamo were there, of course…and Brink's mother, as well as his neighbor in her garden. Somehow, by process of elimination–as in a game of Russian roulette–some were arbitrarily gone and others had remained. Or was it arbitrary? Brink stood in silence, staring at the remaining people, including Jackamo. What was it they all had in common that had caused the Professor to fail at making them disappear? Well, the Professor himself was gone, so Brink reframed his own question. What was it they all had in common that caused them to *remain* just as they were?

Brink wasn't quite sure what the best word was to capture their commonality. Peaceful seemed to fit the description. Whatever it was, they seemed *real* in some way. That was it…they were the only ones remaining because they were living the 'inside-out' lives! No one, including his mother, seemed to be influenced or concerned with what others were thinking about them. He remembered his mom carrying on with her life after his dad had left them, moving steadily through each day without drama, focusing on what needed to be done to keep them both on track.

He looked around at the others, including Jackamo. Each seemed to be absorbed in his or her world in a very real way. Each seemed somehow fully present to their surroundings and each other, as in the case of Olivia's grandparents sitting together in each other's company. It all seemed so glaringly simply and uncomplicated. The Professor had cleared away the distractions of the 'outside-in' people by allowing them, and himself, to return to their nothingness. All that remained were the fully present, authentic beings.

There was one more thing that Brink noticed as he looked around. It was quiet…*really* quiet. The only sound present was the ever so slight rubbing of the cat's head against the chair leg. And, unlike at the airport, Brink could not sense any thoughts filling the room!

Brink took one last look around, and was contemplating walking over to his mother. He wanted to tell her what he had never really expressed to her outwardly before…that he felt bad about his father leaving them, yes; but more importantly, that he really appreciated all that she had done for him…that he *loved* her. But just as he started to walk toward her, Jackamo stepped away from the chair, came over to him and started rubbing the back of his head on Brink's leg. That cat just seemed like he would never get enough of having his ears scratched! He continued, in his characteristically insistent way…just rubbing and rolling his head around against Brink's leg over and over again.

Brink reached down to scratch behind Jackamo's ears. *Good little man,* he thought as he felt the cat's soft, warm fur and then the cold nose pressing up against his hand. Then Jackamo proceeded to walk straight up Brink's leg and across his chest *How bizarre!* he thought as the cat– suspended in the air against him– began kneading his paws back and forth, back and forth, gently pressing them into Brink's chest.

Brink opened his eyes to find himself back on the wicker chair on Olivia's porch, staring into a large set of green eyes as the cat, perched with his hind legs in his lap, stretched out to Brink and continued kneading his paws against his chest.

Brink sat up a bit straighter and took a breath, somewhat in a daze from his deep, unexpected afternoon 'catnap'. It took him a moment of looking around to remember where he was…*who* he was. The dream had been so vivid, so real; yet he knew it was only a dream. Still, there was a message there that he wanted to understand before the dream slipped away. Already he could feel it eluding him, as Jackamo continued to press his forehead against the back of Brink's arm, quietly demanding more ear scratching.

His mother…Brink started to remember that he had been walking toward her when the cat had interrupted and gently awakened him. He wanted to tell her something important. What was it? And what about the others who had been there…both those who had shattered to pieces and those who remained? *Why had some disappeared and some stayed intact?* he asked himself again. *What was the thread here…the message of his dream?* He wanted so desperately to remember!

He was hungry, and he suddenly thought about the second plate of food that Olivia had brought this morning and left on the counter. It was the last piece of pie, she had said. So he got up from the chair and headed for the kitchen….

~ 23 ~

SeCrET iNgrEdIenT

Brink uncovered the foil from the paper plate sitting on the counter and stared at the pie. This was it, the very last piece of that wonderful pie…and Olivia had saved it out for *him*. That fact, in itself, touched him somehow. But then there was the pie itself, of course! He saw the pieces of hard cheddar sitting atop it and knew that he had to eat it warm, so he looked around for the microwave.

Why wasn't it a surprise to him that there wasn't one? He hadn't noticed a TV anywhere either. *Interesting,* he thought to himself. *I guess it's possible to live without some of the modern conveniences I've gotten used to,* he noted to himself. He moved toward the oven, noticed the box of wooden matches next to it, and realized he would have to light it if he wanted to experience that pie warm again like it had been the night before. *Wow, was it just last night that I arrived here?* he thought to himself, as he heard the oven burner catch. *For some reason, it seems like I have been here a lot longer than that,* he pondered, as he slid the pie onto a ceramic plate, placed it on the oven shelf, and sat down at the table to gaze out the window.

As he waited for the pie to warm up, his mind drifted back to his dream again. It seemed that most of the significant recent characters in his life had been in it, as well as some others…like the fear-filled folks at the airport, who Freud would undoubtedly say represented all of his own personal fears. He knew dreams were only metaphors of sorts, and often not even as clear as this one had been with these very specific, recognizable people in it. But one person of significance seemed to be missing…his father. Sure, his dad was dead now, but so were Violet and Tomas, Olivia's grandparents, who had been in it. *What's up with that?* he wondered.

He could smell the aroma of the pie coming from the oven and was already anticipating its taste. In preparation to receive it properly, he went to the fridge to get some of the goat's milk that he knew was there. It wasn't his favorite, but warm pie without milk just didn't seem right to him somehow. As he poured the milk, and pulled the warm pie with melted cheese from the oven, he remembered what Olivia had told him about the secret ingredient in her grandmother's cooking. "Love" was all she had simply said, with a smile.

Maybe that was it. Those in the dream that had remained –rather than crumble and disappear–all seemed to still be carrying love, while those who had disappeared seemed to have been full of fear, anger or other predominantly negative emotions. Yes, he believed that might be the missing piece…one of the key ingredients to a happy life. From within, he could immediately hear his own cynical voice call out:

Duh, you idiot! How corny are you going to get with all of this stuff anyway?

For a glancing moment, he was about to bite and swallow that thought as real, but then he caught himself…yes, some part of him *noticed* that the voice had done its best, as always, to drag him into that negative place.

What was real and true…what was not? Which voices should he be listening to? Which part of himself could he trust? Should he allow himself to be guided by those very comfortable and familiar critical voices that he knew so well, or by those which seemed to originate from some deeper place within? Somehow, in that moment, he knew that the critical voice–although it *appeared* to be coming from inside of him–was really an 'outside-in' voice that he had learned from others. But the latter voice–although not as familiar–was more authentically a part of him which was truly speaking with innate wisdom from the 'inside-out'.[9] He knew with every fiber of his being that he could trust in that very real inner voice right now.

In his mind's eye, Brink reached over and touched the false inner critic's cynical voice… Tap.Tap.Tap. Voila! To his amazement and delight it cracked, shattered and then simply disappeared! He felt relieved…even a bit hopeful. Could he possibly be getting closer to a breakthrough with all of this?

He took a nice, slow, calming breath, closed his eyes, and tasted the first fork full of warm pie. As silly as it seemed, he believed he could actually *taste* the love in the pie! *So,* he thought to himself, *I wonder what the other key ingredients to this whole puzzle are?* He began once again to run through everything that he had been studying and thinking about to solve this plague of thoughts that had been tormenting him for so long.

If Love is one of the possible parts of the solution to living a simple and happy life, what are some of the others? was his focus in that moment. In his mind, he became determined to first eliminate everything that did *not* seem to be serving him in some positive way. The negative emotional pieces–the fear, anger, sadness and shame–definitely did not seem to help overall. *But realistically, a person doesn't just get rid of those with a Tap.Tap.Tap.* he observed.

All of this suddenly seemed way too complicated and overwhelming to him. Dreams seemed to have a way of boiling everything down to a *simple* form. Why not do the same here? Rather than try to get too detailed and figure out every possible solution to all of life's problems at once, he went back to re-examining what his inquiry had covered, in order to identify the basics. *Just name the ingredients and go from there,* he told himself.

There were the core emotions of fear, anger, sadness, shame and joy. Then there was the aspect of the 'outside-in' and 'inside-out' patterns of energy flow. And last, but certainly not least, there was the element of the *thoughts* themselves. *Thoughts, Emotions, Energy Flow…that is as simple as I can possibly get in attempting to identify the key ingredients,* he reminded himself. So where exactly did the element of *Love* fit into this? And–as wonderful as all of this theory was–he knew from his empty experience in graduate school that theory was exactly all it *ever* would amount to unless he could find a way to *apply* it to his life. "The Happy Life Puzzle" is what he decided to call it in that moment. *After all,* he thought, *isn't that what this dilemma is really all about?*

Satisfied with his progress on putting this essential framework in place, Brink focused in on savoring the rest of the pie….

~ 24 ~

†He WaTcheR

Getting up from the table, it dawned on Brink that he hadn't thought even once about getting back in his car and continuing his journey on to the Nevada desert and the Burning Man gathering. He had made great progress in just one long day, getting all the way from Knoxville to the beginning of Nebraska's western panhandle. But with his thoughts continuing to swirl and now finally starting to congeal, he felt like he was on the verge of a breakthrough of some kind. It seemed like slowing down a bit might prove helpful. Besides, it was *he* who had created the agenda of going to Burning Man to begin with. There was no agreement to meet anyone out there at a given time. So couldn't he slow down the pace a bit if he chose to? *Hmmm,* he pondered as he noticed himself going through this process…

> *That thought has a refreshingly different quality than my usual pattern of giving myself a difficult time making these decisions. I wonder what that shift is about.*

Just then, he remembered Olivia mentioning how she sometimes sat in the garden when she was feeling lost;

and 'lost' definitely seemed to pinpoint where he was at in this moment…even though his last observation had a certain element of being very grounded. So he passed back through the living room, pausing for just a few moments to take in the Dark Carobola painting again, then through the doors to the garden. And, just as Olivia had described, the cat followed right behind him….

Brink had no idea what the temperature was, but it felt plenty warm. There was just a bit of shade from the small balcony protruding from the second floor overlooking the garden. The bench was situated perfectly to take advantage of the shade, yet still take in the sunny garden itself and the longer view beyond…so Brink settled in.

As he sat down, more of Olivia's grandmother's words came floating back to him. "Stick to the basics" was part of the advice she had given Olivia about painting. And, even though solving this puzzle called life was not like learning to paint, somehow he felt that advice might still apply. He had the key pieces laid out now…the thoughts, emotions and energy flow connection between them. Then there was the dream and the inside-out piece, along with that secret ingredient, love. Even Jackamo had appeared in the dream and remained. More than likely the cat hadn't disappeared because–like most animals–he was simple, full of love and also had a natural 'inside-out' unselfconscious behavior.

As far as theories went, he felt as if he was back in grad school. Sure, he had a lot of great ideas about all these thought and emotion configurations, but could he ultimately put any of it to *use* to actually *change his life?* It had all just started out as an outlet for his painting. He had wanted to put a new twist into his art, so he had begun to observe people's energy, then categorize and paint them. But the painting had quickly become the least of it all. No, what really took over and consumed him was his own internal struggles and torment…those never-ending voices of self-criticism. So here he was, with this grand scheme put together; but the bottom line was that it was all *academic*. What was he supposed to *do* with all of this information so that it could create a real change in his life?

Rather than help him figure things out, everything had instead gotten more complex and the thoughts and voices in his head had just gotten busier and louder day by day. A sense of futility came over him, as if he were just being swallowed up by it all. Once again he started to feel overwhelmed, as if his sea of thoughts were an endless body of water in which he was drowning, with no hope of land in sight.

As he sat back and looked out at the sky, the sun had already sunken a bit but Brink could still feel the warmth of it radiating into his chest. It felt very soothing. A few clouds were beginning to drift by, and he watched them gently move along with a slow but steady breeze that he could feel brushing his cheeks. Looking at the clear sky helped him empty his mind a bit. During the rare moments when he was able to stop thinking, he felt good. Maybe that was the point of all the meditation that he had attempted a few years back...but overall, he just hadn't clicked with that practice. Sitting still did not seem to be one of his stronger abilities. Right at this moment, however–sitting in this beautiful garden–he actually felt calmer and more peaceful than he had in quite a while…with the exception of figuring out this whole thought craziness thing, of course. *My mind is still racing with this happy life puzzle,* he noticed himself thinking, *but my body itself is starting to feel relaxed.*

He watched the clouds continue to pass by the sun, briefly obscuring it at moments, then returning to its previous brightness and warmth. From out of nowhere it seemed, he began wondering what his mind would be like if it were as calm and clear as the blue sky. There were no clouds–and no thoughts–for the briefest instance…and then just a scattered few…and now the clouds were moving in at a slightly faster pace as the breeze started to pick up a bit.

What if each thought were just like a cloud? he suddenly thought. *What if my basic assumption has been wrong all along about these thoughts plaguing me constantly?* A light bulb went on in Brink's mind as strong as the sun itself!

> *What if I <u>can't</u> ever actually STOP the thoughts? I mean, I am human. We humans simply <u>have</u> thoughts; that's part of the deal. What if all I can do is <u>accept</u> them and <u>watch</u> them as they pass me by?*

But if it's me that is <u>having</u> them, who is it
that is <u>watching</u> them?

The bookmark re-surfaced in his mind…that piece that had come up repeatedly in recent instances. Even Olivia's grandmother had said something that sounded like it at one point. "Don't let the voices talk you in or out of doing your art...or anything else for that matter!" Her grandmother Violet had told her. "It's ok to *notice* the voices," she had taught her, "but in the end you must simply follow your heart. It is the only thing you can always rely on to be the true you."

This 'Noticer'–this 'Watcher' of the voices–was what Brink had caught a glimpse of at the tail end of his drive last night…and then again earlier today. Olivia's grandmother was obviously aware of it as well. It was also a piece that he had heard mentioned in some of the meditation practices way back when, but he never really considered it outside of that context. In fact, there was simply a part of him that–if he paid close enough attention–was an *awareness* of his thinking process that was not the thoughts themselves. So long as he was caught up in the content of each thought–and subsequently caught up in the emotion which that particular set of thoughts was triggering–his perspective was, to some extent, lost. It was like the clouds…actually being *inside the clouds* was not at all the same as him sitting here simply *watching* the clouds–and his thoughts–drift by.

Now that was a thought worth having! Brink said to himself. If all else failed and the thoughts began to plague him, he could always step back and become the *observer* of the thoughts themselves! He had finally realized–only moments before–that he might never be able to actually *stop* the thoughts…that his entire premise of trying to stop the thoughts from rising up was wrong! Instead of hoping to *stop* them, all he really had to do was simply lean back and relax…and *watch* them….

What he now saw clearly was that–rather than be plagued by their actual content and self-criticism–he could instead become the 'Watcher' of his thoughts.[10] When the flood of thoughts began, he could pay attention and focus on simply *noticing* not only when and where they occurred, but also what impact they might be having on his emotions. In fact, he could even *notice and watch his emotions* and the effects they were bringing to him in the moment!

Brink sat back, pleased with his understanding and progress. It sounded like a great plan. He actually felt hopeful that he might escape from years of his tormenting patterns. But still–as he stepped back away from himself– he couldn't help but watch and notice that there was a certain uneasiness beneath his hope….

~ 25 ~

CRACKED OPEN

The feeling that arose for Brink as he settled back to observe his uneasiness was one of somehow being incomplete. His thoughts–and his *watching* of the thoughts themselves as they passed–marked a new awareness that he sensed would help him. At the very least, this would allow him to gain perspective on himself and possibly be released from getting caught up in his own drama. But, as hopeful as this all sounded, his mind kept wandering back to the vividness of his dream, and the picture of his mother once again flashed in front of him.

He recalled how he had been heading toward her to tell her how grateful he felt for her love, and the way that she had *always* supported and encouraged him to be himself. She had left Knoxville a long time ago, and he had never really verbalized anything like this to her. Perhaps now he could actually head west to complete the vision in his dream. He made a promise to himself to seek her out, give her this long-awaited message of gratitude, and re-connect with her. He could feel the sadness rising in him at that very moment; his mother had never remarried, and he knew that in many ways her attention to him was one of the main things that had kept her going all of those difficult years.

It was the vision of his father, however, that continued to elude him. His father's *absence* from the dream–like his absence in Brink's life itself–seemed significant in some way. As he sat reflecting on it, he could feel an even deeper sadness rising up from within his heart. He flashed once again on the father kneeling down to speak to his son at the grocery store, and how he had felt so uneasy in that moment that he actually left the store and stopped his observations for the day. Why? Something deep within him had been triggered…so profound that in that moment he wasn't even aware of how much he was hurting from this picture. At the time he had attributed it to something he might have eaten that was causing him physical distress, but now it was clear that there was much more to it.

He sat on the bench observing this uneasiness rise up inside of him, then reached into his pocket and pulled out the drawing he had tucked away earlier. He unfolded it slowly and just sat there, staring at it for what seemed like an eternity. Then, for the first time, Brink remembered something that he had buried deeply a long time ago. It was back in kindergarten when he had come home with his very first drawings from school. The teacher had told him he had real talent. His mother had been proud of him, taking in his work and praising him for his expressiveness and creativity. He brought home pieces almost daily after that for about a week, relishing in this newfound delight.

Then one day his father came home from his long business trip, took one look at Brink's drawings and had said simply, "What in the hell do you think you're going to accomplish with those? What a waste of time!" And that was the end of the beginning of his art for many, many years. Despite his mother's efforts to encourage him to do more, he simply shut it down, denying that he really enjoyed it.

As far as Brink could remember, most things in his life up to that short period had been full of love and acceptance. He found out soon after those devastating remarks, that his dad had been "let go" of his position at his company. Brink realized now, looking back, that much of his father's remarks were probably just a venting of his displaced frustration. Yet no matter what his mother had said to try to erase the impact of his father's remarks that day, there was no going back.

Things seemed to go downhill quickly in their house after that. Dad was home for a while without work, then came and went from different jobs. Money was always tight and Brink remembered how his birthday had been a little disappointing that year...and the Christmas holiday, too. Somewhere during that time his father started drinking and getting angry a lot...often over what seemed like the smallest little things. Brink's behavior became quieter and more subdued, afraid that if he got too excited about something or said the wrong thing, his Dad might haul off and start yelling again…or even hit him as he occasionally had.

That whole period seemed to last a long, long time, but looking back, Brink figured it was probably about two years. Then one day his Dad had pulled him aside when he dropped him off at school and said:

> "Son, I'm going to be leaving for a while. You be good to your Momma and make something of yourself. Play some sports. Learn a trade. Don't waste your time on any of that art crap. And forget about all that sales crap that I've wasted my life with too...that and a dollar will barely get you a cup of coffee. Just get out there and make some money and be happy."

Brink could feel in his body's memory how he had started to cry, but his father had given him a little shake and finished by saying:

> "You're going to be the man of the house now…and remember what I told you about boys not crying? Well, the same is true for men. You and your momma will be fine."

And with that, he was gone. Brink didn't see or hear from him again for years. He participated in sports and took trades classes like his dad had told him. He wanted his dad to be proud of him when he came back. But, of course, Dad never did return. He asked his mom over and over where his dad lived and if he could go see him. But she wanted no part of that, and certainly didn't want Brink involved with him either.

When Brink was a senior in high school, he decided to track his father down during semester break. Although the Internet was still relatively new at the time, it helped him locate his Dad, who was living in a mid-size city a few hundred miles away. He had mustered up the courage to go and surprise him, but that turned out to be a bit of a disaster. His Dad had acted happy to see him, and they had gone to get some lunch to get to know each other a bit. At his dad's suggestion they had a celebration toast, but one thing led to another and it was clear to Brink after his dad's third beer at lunchtime that there was an issue there. He had told himself he would be open and not judge him; but it was pretty damn hard to see his dad almost drink himself under the table right before his eyes.

All in all, it had been a very disheartening visit. He had pictured that sharing everything he accomplished in school would make his Dad proud, including being on track for a basketball scholarship to college. But nothing turned out like the picture he had been holding in his head all those years. Shortly after that, Brink lost his enthusiasm for basketball and most of his science and trade classes as well. He didn't drop out of school, but instead starting taking psychology classes. Somehow he needed to satisfy himself and try to understand how a life like his father's could turn sour so quickly.

Now, sitting here twenty years later, the light bulb was finally coming on for Brink. It suddenly seemed so obvious looking back on it all. He had strived and strived to become the man his father described that last day he dropped him off at school. How he had let his father's words guide and influence him without even realizing it for so many years!

He got angry just thinking about it...his father's voice rising in his head over and over again as Brink had made what he thought were his own decisions along the way. His mother had always encouraged him to listen to his heart, just as Olivia's grandmother had said. All these years he had *thought* he was doing just that. But now he could see that what he was really doing rather than following his heart was to *avoid the pain in his heart* from his father abandoning him and his mother. Damn his dad! Why couldn't he have just stuck it out with their family and made the best of things?

The pain of these realizations and the impact of Brink's father leaving him were suddenly too much to bear. His head felt like it was splitting open, cracking right down the middle. His heart was beating rapidly, and he was starting to sweat profusely. He closed his eyes and just felt like screaming. Why had his father left him? Maybe if he had been a better boy, things might have been different. Didn't his father love him? Wasn't he *worthy* enough? *Lovable* enough? *Perfect* enough just the way he was?

Brink suddenly heard a rumbling as the sky grew darker. He looked up to see the clouds growing thicker and gathering into a dense mass, now completely obscuring the sun behind it. He felt a cold downdraft of air rush over him, and a chill ran up his body. In that moment, for the first time, he noticed Jackamo sitting on a small wooden crate in front of the bench. He watched as the cat, detecting the oncoming rain, jumped down from the top and took his place sitting inside the safety of the crate's shelter, but where he could still be in full view.

As Brink watched the cat's large green eyes, the small black slits in them seemed to grow larger and darker each second. Sure enough, the green in his eyes got smaller, the long cat slits expanded and simultaneously Brink's heart felt like it was exploding from the pain of all of the memories of his father. The pain in his heart grew until it was unbearable, and Brink let out a wail and began to sob uncontrollably as he felt a fiery release from deep within. In that very instant, Jackamo looked at him and arched his back in that cat-like way and let out a deep howl…and then…CRACK!...a huge strike of lightning hit the tower and a burst of rain was released from the sky.

Brink continued to sob from within as the rain poured down upon him. All the while, Jackamo sat and stared at him, as if to absorb the pain that Brink was releasing from the abysmal wound that had been opened inside of him. There was another crack of thunder, a bit off in the distance, accom-panied by another flash of lighting across the field…then another downdraft of air, this time a bit warmer. As the warm air washed over Brink, he looked out and observed the sudden storm moving away as quickly as it had materialized. Olivia's words echoed in Brink's mind: "Jackamo will keep an eye on you, won't you good little man?"

Brink felt completely drained...empty yet somehow full at the same time. Between the rain drenching him from outside and his tears flowing from within, he actually felt refreshed and cleansed in a strange kind of way. His mind flashed on the man crying at the cemetery. Brink could not remember ever crying like this before. In fact, he really couldn't remember crying at all since one time as a young child when he had fallen off his bike and skinned his knee badly. He hadn't even cried at his father's funeral a couple of months ago. But he had definitely cried for his dad just now. The pain he felt was as if his heart had cracked open. He had no idea that all that energy had been kept inside of him...*stored inside his heart.*

The sky was still thick with clouds. As Brink sat there quietly, the clouds began to slowly drift and part. They were still bundled in dark masses, but the light from the sun was beginning to peek around their dark edges. For a fleeting moment, as the clouds shifted, Brink swore to himself that he saw the shape of a heart in the dark clouds, with the brilliant light from the sun behind caressing its edges....

~ 26 ~

Sleep-living or Awake?

As the minutes passed, the light breeze seemed to push the clouds along. Then the darker rain-filled clouds passed and were slowly replaced by a lighter, cumulus type. They were almost translucent, and Brink could see the clear silhouette of the round sun right through them, even though he couldn't see its actual direct bright light. The spaces between the light clouds grew greater and the brightness of the sun grew stronger as it shone just for a moment between the thinning clouds. He continued to watch and feel the warmth of the sun as its time behind the clouds grew less and the larger spaces allowed the sun to shine brightly for greater periods of time. Soon the sky was almost free of clouds, with only an occasional few passing by to momentarily obstruct its brightness.

Brink closed his eyes again. He could feel the warmth of the sun on his face...and on his heart. *He could feel the warmth coming from within his heart.* How long his heart had been storing all of that pain surrounding his father leaving!

As the sun warmed him, his mind returned to what he had been thinking about before. The clouds were like his thoughts drifting by…and the sun was like his heart. Somehow it had been hidden all of this time behind the darkness of his constant thoughts and self-criticisms. He had been keeping himself in this self-inflicted bondage for years. In a certain way, he had actually managed to keep his father close by him, by allowing all of his father's messages to stay so present in Brink's mind. How ironic! All of those negative voices were actually Brink's way of *loving* his father by keeping his dad and those messages close to himself!

Brink looked down at the picture sitting in his lap...the colors all running together now from the rain having drenched it. That message from his father at the bottom was smudged but still legible,

I l ve yo son.

D d

It was no wonder that he had felt so much conflict around his own artistic process and resulting works...especially the paintings. He was trying to follow his heart and paint, but the voices of his dad kept telling him that painting was a worthless activity had continued to surface. Yet he couldn't let go of the voices, because that would be like letting go of his dad himself. No, he had to keep those voices present, as conflicting as they were, if he wanted to hold onto his love for his father. There was no way he could do both without the inner turmoil of those two opposing forces showing up…following his heart and his passion for painting from the inside-out, and listening to the negative messages from his father coming from the outside-in in the form of those self-criticizing thoughts in his head…what a setup for self-sabotage!

On some level Brink realized in this moment–sitting on the bench with the sun once again warming him–that he had simply *shut down* his heart. His love for his father, like so many of his other feelings along the way, had been stored as locked up energy in his heart! His internal voices and self-criticisms, and his outright cynicism at times, had all been clouding over his true self. His ability to *feel* his emotions as a whole had been shut down for so long that he had completely lost perspective on what was real versus what was living in his head.

The divine irony of it all was that his father apparently had the same inability to express his feelings and his love for Brink. Yet at some point he had written this message to Brink on this picture. If only he had found this years ago!

Yet all of this wasn't just about his father. No, he had gone all the way with this one. In truth he had never really opened up to Rachel completely either. Sure, they spent lots of time together, but neither of them was ever vulnerable in the way that he was feeling right now. Their relationship was always more of a struggle…her working to convince him to become a certain way; he going along with it for a while to please her, then quietly resisting and resenting her more and more until everything had finally come to a head.

As Brink sat there absorbing one after another of these pieces falling into place, he suddenly felt sorry for his dad. He still didn't understand exactly why his father had left them rather than stay and fight for a better life. He did have a pretty good sense–from his own first-hand experience at the end of high school and into college–that the heavy drinking had served as an escape. But fortunately Brink had overcome that crutch, whereas his father apparently never had. Brink had never really known his own grandfather, but he wondered what messages his father may have been living with inside his own head that his grandfather had passed along to his son in the same way.

A wave of forgiveness came over him. His father had probably done the best that he knew how to, living with whatever voices that had been handed down to him. The picture of his father as a young five year old listening to *his* own father criticizing him suddenly popped into Brink's mind. He wished he could talk to his father in that moment, and tell him how much he really loved and missed him, but his dad was gone now. *That's OK,* thought Brink to himself…

> *I get it now. Maybe one day I will have kids of my own and break this crazy pattern that's been handed down to me….*

Then another wave of forgiveness and compassion came over him regarding Rachel. She probably had also done the best she could, he thought…and then he suddenly had a similar feeling about his old corporate boss. All of them, just like him, had more than likely inherited a lifetime of voices of their own…powerful and convincing, yet sad in a certain kind of way….

Brink felt an inner peace rise up within him like never before. The waves of thoughts that had been plaguing him for so many years seemed to have magically transformed into waves of forgiveness and compassion suddenly washing over him as well. He felt relieved and amazingly refreshed. It was now as clear as the blue sky itself that he could *choose* which voices to listen to. Yes, he could *watch* and *notice* not only his thoughts, but the flow of energy between them and that magical storage compartment known as his heart!

Yet a part of him also felt sad for all the years that he had wasted living his life from the outside-in, following the voices and coaxing of others wanting him to be someone that he naturally wasn't…succumbing to the patterns of thoughts that had kept him living in the shadow of his father. Could he forgive *himself* for those lost years and move on? Could he find it in his newfound heart to let go of those unrecoverable years and start fresh again?

The answer he heard from his *own* voice coming from within was a resounding *"YES!"* His dream had helped him to see clearly that all was *not* lost. There were those who apparently had managed to free themselves of their conflicting voices by living their lives from the inside-out, with their hearts leading the way…those who had not shattered into pieces, but had remained perfectly whole at the illusionist Professor's Tap.Tap.Tap. And now he could consciously *choose* to join those who lived with real love and do the same. If he didn't wake up to this new way of living now, he would surely slip unconsciously back to sleep. And if that happened, there was no doubt that those voices of his father would continue to live on and guide him unknowingly as they had for so long. He might as well fall back asleep and bury himself with his father!

No, he had had enough of living unconsciously and allowing the voices of others to rule his life! Perhaps he should make up a word for it, just as Olivia had done for the Dark Carobola. "Sleep-living" was the term that came to his mind. And then the famous phrase he had read from the poet Rumi rang in his head, "Don't go back to sleep!"[11] *"YES!"* proclaimed Brink to himself, once again…

> *The time has finally come for me to WAKE UP! It's time for me to live my life consciously…to make choices with an open heart. I need to listen to my true inner voice, not to the voices of all the others telling me what I <u>should</u> be doing, who I'm <u>supposed</u> to be, what's <u>worth</u> doing, or–for that matter– what <u>I'm</u> worth!*

At least he now had hope for himself that it was not too late…hope that had come, ironically, from his dream state. But how long, he began to wonder, had all of this energy been stored there...in his heart? When had all of this begun? He started to trace back in his thoughts to the time when he first began to really shut down and pull away from everyone…from life itself in a certain way. But then his *Watcher* appeared and noticed that all of his energy was coming from the thinking in his head once again. He caught himself and realized that–more than anything–the important thing here was to not get lost in those thoughts in his head again. In fact, *that was exactly what had gotten him to this point to begin with!*

The really big piece for him was the realization that his heart had *closed* at some point, trapping the energy of his true feelings inside of him for a long, long time. And it was the abundance of thoughts–piling up like the dark clouds themselves–that had covered over his heart and ability to *feel* his feelings. All of his heart's warmth and love simply buried by his incessant thoughts, questioning and self-criticisms for so many years…all to cover up the pain of losing his father! He must have used this same process unconsciously to pull away from Rachel and– now that he finally admitted it–to pull away from much of the world itself. All of those years of not *feeling* things! But now, with the forgiveness he was granting himself, he felt so much freer, alive and awake!

There was no going back…no more sleep-living for Brink! He was simply here NOW…*AWAKE!* All he could do was *move on* and be grateful that all of the pain from his past had somehow been released. His heart felt truly *open* for the first time. The feeling was almost indescribable, and quite foreign to him. His heart was emptier than he could ever remember, which at first felt sad to him; yet somehow at the same time, he felt joyful. *Or maybe,* the thought seemed to arise from somewhere in the depths of Brink's consciousness, *my heart is now ready to be filled.* He suddenly knew with certainty that because his heart was no longer aching with his buried pain, it–no, *he*–was now *ready to receive* in a new way….

Brink had one last realization as he let out a long slow sigh of relief…*avoiding* pain was not the goal. In fact, that was exactly what he had been doing all along by burying it rather than facing it directly! Instead, he needed to make the conscious choice to allow himself to *feel* the pain in a fully awakened way. He must be sure that his heart remained *open*…even if it was to experience pain rather than love. Only by allowing himself to fully experience and *feel* what was true in the moment could he keep the energy *flowing* through his heart rather than allowing it to become trapped once again.

I do believe I get it now, Brink said to himself, feeling a tremendous sense of having arrived at his destination…or perhaps, having arrived at the start of a new path on the next leg of his journey….

Just keep my heart open and the energy of my true emotions flowing–whether pleasure or pain–and my thoughts and voices will not pile up like the clouds to darken and cover up my life spirit…my Love….

~ 27 ~

hoMe aGaIn

"Hello!" he heard Olivia call from inside the house. "Brink, are you still here?"

Still in a bit of a daze, Brink started to rise from the bench when out walked Olivia into the garden.

"Why look at you…you're all drenched, for Pete's sake! Looks like you got caught in that downpour."

"Uh, yes, I guess so…" he stammered.

"How are you feeling? Did you get a bit of rest?"

Olivia's words echoed in Brink's head for a few moments. "How are you *feeling?*" is what she had asked him. As simple as that sounded, he was aware that the question itself was directed at his whole being…not just what he had been *thinking* about, or what he had been *doing* the whole time she had been back at work. A huge smile broke out across his face. "I am feeling wonderful!" is what he heard and felt coming from inside and out. He let out a bit of a laugh and continued, "I guess I'm feeling a bit drenched and wet, but pretty damn good!"

She paused just a moment, looking at him with her head angled just a bit. "You seem…well, a bit *different*…sort of more *awake* than before. What's that?" she added, pointing to the drawing clutched in his fingers.

"Oh, it's just a silly little drawing. I'll tell you about it later." Brink laughed again. *If she only knew where my mind and heart have been this afternoon!* was all he could think, saying nothing more.

"There's still a bunch of Grandpa's clothes in one of the closets. If I get you a dry shirt to wear, do you think you might do me a small favor?" she asked.

"What's that?" he replied.

"Well, this may sound sort of silly to you. Most of what I paint is landscapes and things that just come up for me. I don't usually do people. But there is something about the look on your face right now that I can't quite put my finger on. If you think you could sit still for maybe twenty minutes or so, I would love to see if I can capture a bit of that."

"That's fine with me. I have no plans at the moment," he said.

"OK, go ahead on in there and I'll be right back with that shirt!" and she disappeared as suddenly as she had arrived, as if whisked away by a force greater than herself.

Brink made his way to the studio, and as he sat on the stool awaiting her return, he smiled inwardly to himself. Olivia was just so…well, he wasn't quite sure how to describe her really…'refreshing' might be a suitable adjective. Whatever it was about her, she simply had an unhesitating way of speaking and expressing herself that seemed simple, honest and open. It was so straightforward that it was almost foreign to him. All that time he had spent with Rachel he had so often found himself to be guarded in some way; but conversations with Olivia just seemed to flow right along....

He began to think again about his interactions with her at the diner last night and at the kitchen table earlier that morning. She seemed so amazingly attentive. It wasn't put on or self-conscious in any way whatsoever; she simply seemed to be listening to him with her entire being, then responding from a completely non-judgmental place of natural curiosity. There didn't appear to be a hidden agenda...just a refreshing openness that he rarely, if ever, could recall experiencing on an everyday basis with other people he had known. The only other person that even came close was his friend Damien who, although open and honest with him, was in general very cynical and judgmental about the world. Olivia was definitely unique in more ways than one. It was as if she didn't let any of her own clouds of thinking or pre-conceived notions block out any part of being with him. She just seemed so amazingly *present.*

He looked around her studio and remembered that before leaving he had thrown away ALL of his art and supplies, except for just a few pieces now in the back seat of his car. But seeing all that was around him and feeling it resonate from within him, he understood that creativity was so profoundly a part of his nature that to leave it behind was impossible. The supplies were just more material things that could be gotten anytime; it was the *energy* within him that would never go away.

Just then, Olivia returned to the studio. "Here you go," she said, tossing the slightly tattered plaid flannel shirt to him from a few feet away. "This was one of my grandfather's favorites," she continued, "…it's what I like to call *lovingly worn!"*

Brink slipped off his wet shirt and replaced it with the dry one, thinking about Olivia's little play on the words 'lovingly worn.' He couldn't tell if she had intentionally made the double meaning from the word 'worn' or not, but somehow he guessed that she had. Certainly her grandfather had worn it lovingly until it was almost worn out. But with Olivia, it often seemed that things just came out of her so naturally that there weren't any hidden meanings behind her words. *Either way, it's pretty cute,* Brink thought to himself *…and so is she.*

Brink sat quietly for about the first ten minutes, as Olivia worked whatever bit of magic that spoke to her through her brushes. It was only after he sat for a while that it dawned on him suddenly that his mind–for once–had actually been quite still. He felt very peaceful overall. Gradually, he felt a question naturally rise up from within…"Can I ask you something?" he said turning his head back toward her for a moment where she stood behind the easel.

"Sure, so long as you turn your head back and don't move!" she bounced back.

"It's about your cat, Jackamo." Brink said.

"What about him? Didn't he do a good job keeping an eye on you today?"

"Well, yes, he did. Somehow I think he did even more than that, but I can't quite put my finger on it," he responded with a puzzled twist to his voice. "He seems kind of…well, *other-worldly* or something." Out of the corner of his eye Brink could see Olivia toss her head back and then heard her let out a loud laugh.

"Oh, don't even go there," she chuckled. "Grams and I tried to figure that one out for the longest time, and finally decided to just let sleeping dogs lie…or cats, as it is in Jackamo's case."

"What do you mean by that?" Brink asked.

"Well, you see…Jackamo sort of appeared from nowhere in the barn out back one day a few months after Grandpa passed away. Mind you, there are plenty of strays in the area, but this town's not very big…in case you hadn't noticed. In fact, technically, we are not even a town."

"There's a post office, isn't there?" Brink noted.

"Sort of…but not really," she continued. "That's just Mr. Kosek's way of keeping busy. You see, most of this little town–if you want to call it that–is just a cluster of Czech family and friends that started building near each other. He runs the little emporium, too. Basically, he gathers up the mail once a week and makes a run over to McCook where the real post office is. We're not really official enough to be on the map, I guess."

"So…you were saying…about the cat, I mean?"

"Oh right!" she laughed again. "I guess I lost my train of thought there for a minute…I must be catching a bit of that from you! What I mean to say is that everyone sort of knows everyone else and what goes on around here, including the critters. And it seems that when Jackamo appeared, he was a different color than the rest of the strays and no one else had seen him before. So I guess me and Grams just figured that somehow Grandpa had kind of sent him here to keep an eye on us both, if that makes any sense to you at all."

Brink hesitated. He wasn't quite sure what he believed, but he did feel somehow that this particular cat was far from ordinary.

Before he had formed any response, Olivia simply finished with, "Sometimes we just can't really *know* about certain things, as much as we may be curious. We just *love* Jackamo. And you know that old expression 'Curiosity killed the cat?'" she asked.

"Sure, I've heard that one before," Brink replied.

"Well, truth of the matter is," said Olivia pausing to toss her hands up in the air a bit, "we'd rather give up our curiosity than lose our cat!"

Brink turned and looked at her, then over at Jackamo, who was sitting in the corner listening. "I guess you're right enough about that. The important thing is that he's just *here,* I guess. And I'm not sure quite how, but I think he helped me out quite a bit today."

"It's all the Love he carries," said Olivia, stopping to put her brushes down. She took a slow breath, glanced at Brink and then back to the canvas again and said, "Well, I think I've gotten all I care to for today on capturing you.

Maybe we can finish this up a bit later on?" She smiled and turned, not waiting for his response.

What's next? thought Brink, as he got up from the portrait stool and followed her into the kitchen. Then, as if to answer his own question, he said to himself:

Feels just like I'm home again....

~ 28 ~

PHoEbe anD tHe fALcOn

"So are you feeling rested enough to head off to this Burning Man thing you were talkin' about? You never did really say much about what that was anyway," she said as she rustled through the pots under the kitchen sink.

"Well, it's kind of hard to describe if you haven't been there before. I mean…it's different, not for everyone really." He replied. "It's just a lot of creative people sort of gathered out in the middle of the Nevada desert sharing whatever they have. They pretty much have to haul everything they need onto the site, even their water."

"Never heard of it, but it sure sounds like a lot of work. There must be *something* more to it to attract all of those people out into the middle of nowhere," she observed.

"Yes, it's absolutely amazing!" exclaimed Brink, with more energy than Olivia had seen in him since she had met him. "It's hard to describe in words," he continued, "but let's just say that it's a *very* inspiring place. Some even say that Burning Man *is* the water in the desert. I must say that, for me, it does sort of quench my creative thirst…like the water you gave me yesterday when my throat was so dry. But then again," he continued after a thoughtful pause, "I'm pretty inspired just being *here* and seeing all of what *you've* done with *your* art!"

Olivia seemed to blush for just a moment. Brink took in the soft light coming through the kitchen window, enhancing her inward glow even more. Her skin was amazingly smooth and without a single blemish. "Who knows," he said with just a slight glimmer in his eye, "maybe someday you'll make it out there to experience it for yourself."

"That might be nice. But right now the only place I need to be going is out to the barn to milk my goat Phoebe. I got kind of a late start this morning after getting you back here and settled in last night, and I didn't have a chance to milk her out. She'll be just about bustin' her bag if I don't get out there pretty soon!" she exclaimed. "I was going to milk her first thing when I got home, but the expression on your face was just too…well…*intriguing* to pass up. What happened out here today, if you don't mind my askin'?"

"Honestly," he said looking at her blankly, "I'm not sure that I can really say. I mean, I'm not religious or anything like that, but I had an experience that just sort of opened me up in a way. I'm still trying to get a handle on it."

"Well, I'm happy to listen when it comes to you. Whatever it was, I think it did you some good!" she said, half laughing again, as she strolled out of the kitchen with milking pail in hand. Olivia glanced back over her shoulder adding, "C'mon now…we can't keep a good goat waiting!"

Brink felt his heart flutter just a bit. *Those blue-green eyes have to be some of the sexiest on the planet,* he thought to himself, as he followed her out to the barn.

"This won't take long," she said. "Phoebe's a Saanen, by the way, named for the Saanen valley in Switzerland. They're one of the most productive and easy to care for breeds for milking. But I got her because I love her all white, soft and silky coat. Isn't she just beautiful?"

"I guess so. I don't know much about goats, really. But didn't she have to have some kids for her to be milking right now?" he asked, looking around for a sign of her little ones.

"Sure, she had a couple about six months ago. I traded them out to a farmer down the road for some fresh beef a while back. You can keep milking them for quite some time, but once you slow that down she'll start drying up pretty quick. I've usually got more than I need. I make some into cheese; I bring some into the diner…that kind of thing."

Brink looked around the barn. The goat stall was just a fenced off area in the back corner with a dirt floor and a small doorway of sorts leading to the outside pen. The rest of the barn was about a story and a half tall, with a loft for storage. It had a cement floor and a lot of really nice shelving and work benches along the far wall. Over to the side was a big object under a tarp. "Is that the

Falcon?" he asked curiously, slowly walking in that direction.

"Sure is!" piped up Olivia, with her head pressed gently against the goat's ribs as she continued to milk her. "Go ahead…pull that tarp off of there. You can try to start her up if you'd like. I haven't turned her over in quite some time though."

Brink meandered over to the car and slowly pulled the tarp off and set it to the side. He stood back and took in the car. It faced outward, and sat as if ready to rocket out of the barn at a moment's notice. It was in almost mint condition…a rich burgundy with cream colored leather upholstery, plenty decent looking whitewall tires, and a matching burgundy ring around the edges of the wheel rims.

Compared to what he was driving, this beauty was truly a gem. He'd been having a number of issues with his engine and now the air conditioning had gone out. But mainly, he knew that the body was going to need a fair amount of work at some point soon. And here–by some strange coincidence of the Universe–sat this almost distant cousin of his car…a most amazing specimen of an automobile indeed!

"It's just about the same color as the barn roof," he called over to her, wondering to himself if that were also a coincidence. Sometimes he had the strange feeling that there really were no such things as 'coincidences'; yet that was a whole other tangent that he, once again, simply decided to 'bookmark' for a later time.

"I know it is. Gramps just loved this car and that color; he picked that roof color on purpose just to remind himself of the car from a distance when he was coming in from the fields on his tractor. She glanced over to the other corner of the rear wall where an old hand-crank narrow front end John Deere B stood idle. Well don't just stand there," she said calling playfully over her shoulder to him from the goat stall. "The key's in the ignition. Pull open the barn door and see if she starts!"

Brink didn't hesitate for even a moment. He tugged on the tall sliding barn door and pulled it back, and the light from the late afternoon sun made the Falcon glow even more gloriously. He opened the door and eased behind the wheel of the burgundy beauty, pumped the gas a few times and turned the key. It started to turn over, so he knew the battery was probably fine, but it wouldn't quite catch. "Is there gas in it?" he called over to her, straining to see the fuel gauge with the sun in his eyes.

"Should be…but there's a can over there with a bit in it," she said motioning her head. "Why don't you just dump a little in the carburetor? That usually gets it going."

Brink popped open the hood, took off the air cleaner cover and spilled about half a cup of gas in the carburetor. Then he got back in, pumped the pedal a few more times and the Falcon fired right up.

"I told you she'd start up," said Olivia, walking over with the milk pail in her hands, now full from Phoebe's offerings. "I got almost a quart and a half from her today!

I'll go toss this in the fridge and we can take her out for a spin. You game?"

"But I didn't see any plates on it," said Brink.

She threw back her head and laughed again. "We don't need plates to take her for a test spin. Why, the only one around here that would stop us anyway is Ol' Chester the County Sheriff. All I can imagine he would ticket us for is me refusing to sell him the car! He's been after me for it ever since Gramps passed away. There's a hand pump over there under the work bench if you want to put a little more air in this one," she said pointing to the driver's side distinctively low front tire. "I'll be back in just a few minutes...."

~ 29 ~

full~Out!

Brink pumped up the tire and eased the Falcon out of the barn. Except for a bit of a hole in the muffler, the engine itself sounded smooth and even. Before he knew it, Olivia was back and was jumping into the passenger seat. "Alright, let's do it!" She let out a fun-filled shriek and off they went....

"Go on up here to the corner, make a left and head right out of town. There's a nice straightaway up there and we can really put some wind in this puppy," she said.

Brink did just as she said and within a few minutes they were headed down a long road that faded into the horizon. "Let her rip!" said Olivia.

"Are you sure?" asked Brink.

"Sure! Why not? You only live once, you know!" she cried out in delight.

Brink stepped on the gas and the Falcon accelerated, popping just a few times before really picking up speed. He looked over and Olivia had her head out the window with her hair blowing back in the wind. She was laughing with the sheer delight of a child! He pressed on the accelerator and before he knew it the red needle on the white speedometer was hitting 90, with the car just purring in the wind.

Olivia let out a huge "Woo Hoooo!" and turned to him absolutely beaming. He slowed the car down after it had peaked in speed and she turned to him and said, "See, she hasn't lost her pep a bit. Hey, are you hungry? I sure am. Let's head back and I'll make us a quick little dinner… unless you're heading out tonight?" she asked as she looked over toward him.

Brink thought he detected a bit of disappointment in her voice. "Uh…well, it is getting a little late to start out." He paused…"I might just take you up on that wicker couch offer one more time. I guess I fell asleep in the chair this afternoon for a while after you went back to work. But I'm beginning to feel more like myself. It's been a good day."

He paused for a moment, as if thinking of what to say next. "Sure, I'm hungry…let's go!" he suddenly bellowed. Then he slammed on the brakes, cranking the wheel as he guided it into a masterful U-turn in the middle of the long stretch of road. "Yeeee Haaaw!" Brink screamed out, as he looked over at her with a huge smile on his face, let the car fly full-out, and simultaneously gave her a gentle slap on her thigh. "I know how to have fun, too, you know!" Then he punched the gas pedal and off they sped, laughing and whooping in their shared delight….

~ 30 ~

LiNguINe wIth lOvE

By the time they returned to the house, they were both laughing almost continuously. Brink had been filling Olivia in a bit more about the goings on at Burning Man. He was probably bending her mind almost as much as she had shifted his, taking in all of her complex artwork set against her lack of formal training and simple lifestyle. She also shared a few more short Jackamo stories, which he listened to in amazement.

Olivia looked around the kitchen for a few minutes, then grabbed a big onion from a wire basket hanging to the side and asked him to start cutting it up. Then she disappeared again for about five minutes and came back clutching an apron full of fresh veggies from the garden. She put a big stainless pot on the stove, washed her hands–along with a bunch of tomatoes–then literally squeezed them into pieces over the pot, almost squealing with delight. Brink watched her with almost as much delight as she seemed to be having herself. As he observed her sensuously squashing the last of the tomatoes, one of them slipped through her fingers and fell onto the floor, splattering in every direction. "Silly me! Guess I've got a ways to go before I make the perfect sauce…should have been a bit more careful I suppose," she said laughingly. "Oh well…have to move on…no sense living in the *'should haves.'* I just love making a good, fun sauce!" she declared, as she leaned down to wipe up the mess on the floor.

Brink continued to observe her as she cleaned up the spilled tomatoes. He drank in all of her strikingly simple yet alluring feminine aspects with his eyes; but even more noticeable than that, what he realized was that she actually seemed just as *delighted* to clean up the mess as she was in making the sauce itself! It was as if she made no 'good' or 'bad' association with any particular action…rather, she seemed simply *present* to whatever was happening in the moment in a joyful way.

When she finished, she grabbed a big hefty iron skillet, put a couple more large yellow onions in it, shoved it toward Brink and said in a stern yet soft manner, "You best stop staring and start sautéing, Mr. Brink, or we'll never get this sauce made." Finally, she peeled and crushed a few cloves of garlic, tossed them in with the onions, poured a bit of olive oil on them and starting looking around again.

"What are you making?" he asked.

"Not quite sure yet, but starting with garlic and onions is always a sure thing. And with all the tomatoes out there in the garden, I thought it best to cook some of them up…or else they'll just rot and be no good to anyone. Gramps wouldn't like me wasting all that precious water on these veggies for no reason at all."

"What else are you planning on putting in here?" he asked, stirring the onions as they began to caramelize.

"Oh, I guess maybe some of this zucchini, some of these green and red peppers and maybe just a few carrots. You're not one of those vegetarians, are you? 'Cause I've got some of that fresh ground beef that I was telling you I traded for in the fridge…just took it out of the deep freeze the other day. How about we just toss that in and put on some linguine noodles to cook?"

"Sounds delicious…but aren't you missing something?"

"What's that?" she said, looking at him a bit puzzled.

"The LOVE!" cried Brink, as he gently stirred the onions and garlic.

They both laughed, catching each other's eyes for just long enough to drink each other in.

"Do you drink wine?" Olivia asked him. "I mean, I'm not what you'd call a regular drinker like some, but I like to every once in a while when it feels like…well, a special occasion." She turned away from him, as if she was a bit embarrassed by having made the last remark.

"Not as much as I used to…but I'll have a glass if you're going to open a bottle…although I didn't exactly notice a liquor store here in this big town," he added, raising his pitch at the end as if to ask a question.

"Oh, I can explain that. You see my grandparents apparently really enjoyed their Czech wines and there are still a half dozen bottles in the wine cellar," she said laughingly.

"You have a wine cellar?" Brink remarked back to her.

"Well, I like to think of it as one. Gramps apparently dug it out years ago because he knew no wines could keep with the hot weather we have around here." She walked over to the corner of the kitchen and knelt down, lifting up a barely detectable hatchway hidden almost perfectly amidst the wood flooring. Then she leaned over and reached down into the hole until her arm practically disappeared up to her shoulder, with her butt raised up in the air ever so slightly. Brink couldn't take his eyes off of her, as she struggled just a bit, letting out a slight, quiet groan.

"Here's one," she said, as she pulled a dusty bottle up from beneath the floor. She set it down so she could close the lid of the hidden 'wine cellar', and as she lowered it to its resting place she set her other hand on the floor to take a breath, ending up for a moment on all fours. She turned her head up slightly and looked back over at him saying, "It says it's a Cabernet from Moravia."

Brink observed her on all fours for that fleeting moment, and something within him stirred as it hadn't in a long, long time. She was almost cat-like and, he had to admit to himself, extremely sexy. Suddenly his earlier thoughts of being five years too old for her and a few pounds overweight seemed irrelevant…even age itself struck him as a ridiculous concept. "Sounds perfect," Brink replied softly.

"Here, do you think you could work on opening this?" she asked, holding the bottle up to him, still kneeling on the floor.

"Sure," he said, as he reached for the bottle with one hand and held out his other to help her up. She glanced at him with the warmest look, in what seemed to be simultaneously both an awkward, yet perfectly comfortable, moment; then they went back to work on the sauce.

What eventually emerged from the iron skillet was the most delicious sauce that Brink had ever tasted. She had tossed in the fresh beef, not worrying about the traditional meatball formula, then added in fresh basil and oregano from her stash of garden herbs, along with some other ready veggies. The flavor was so incredibly full that Brink felt as if he were eating a gourmet meal, rather than a simple dish. *Must just be all the Love in it,* he thought to himself as they polished off their plates.

Brink couldn't remember experiencing a day so full of joy and laughter since he had gone to the carnival with his Mom years ago. The afternoon and evening had flowed by with such a natural exchange of relaxed energy between the two of them. Time seemed to both stand still and simultaneously stretch out and last an eternity. He thought back to his observations of the Laughter Yoga participants, and remembered how he somehow hadn't been able to bring himself to the same place of joy that he had seen them relish in. Yet now, in this most pleasant and yet simplest of days, everything seemed to connect and flow naturally between he and Olivia. *Could it be that easy?* he pondered. *What was so different all of a sudden?*

My heart... Brink reminded himself happily...

> *I do believe it somehow opened up magically in that garden today....*

~ 31 ~

OpeN hEaRT

After dinner they sat out on the porch swing with another glass of wine, just in time to watch the sun start to settle over the horizon. It was a large, glowing ball of red…slowly melting over the gentle hills in the distance.

For the first time that he could remember in his entire life, Brink felt...well, *joyful*, was actually the simplest way to describe it. He had been happy before at various times, but there was something profoundly different about what he was feeling in this moment. It was an almost bottomless joy that he felt resonating down to the core of his being. He thought about what felt different this time. He remembered feeling happy and proud way back when he had brought those first drawings home to show his mother. That was a happiness surrounding that particular instance; there was, of course, nothing like a child's innocent happiness. But thinking back, it was quite clear to him that that feeling was tied not only to his drawings, but also to the recognition and love that came from his mother. But his joy and happiness had disappeared when his father had made those comments about his useless drawings. The question was, "Where had his joy gone?"

He saw it so clearly now, like the clouds parting and the sun coming out from behind them. He felt the glow of the sunset on him, and realized that he had *buried* his core joy years ago with that rejection from his father. And, he had covered it up even more deeply when his father passed away.

It was true that he appeared to be happy at certain moments–such as during some of his sports victories, or at times when he had *accomplished* something, or when he had *done* something like sell one of his paintings for a premium price. But other than that, his few recollections of happiness were actually tied to those times when he had cut the cord to something–*released himself*–and felt freedom again...like when he was let go from the corporate sales job. Thinking back on those few times of fleeting happiness, he saw clearly now that those instances were actually tied to either a *receiving* of recognition or a *releasing* from something. In both cases there was an *external* element to the resulting happiness. What he felt now, though, was profoundly different.

Olivia shifted a bit on the swing and slid just a bit closer to Brink, pointing at the red glowing sky without saying anything.

Yes, he admitted to himself that finding Olivia was very special. Whether or not they continued on together, the real gift was in her showing him the path *of a different way to live his life.* She hadn't said a word about what he should or shouldn't do…so unlike Rachel and some of his other friends. No, she had simply been *who she was,* and allowed him to be the same. She had shown him by example what a life of living fully and of loving the world around oneself could look like. By simply *being herself* and being fully engaged with everything and everyone around her, she seemed to magically flow…to create, to love, to laugh and to have true joy in her life!

Brink suspected that she—like most people in the world—probably had issues that would occasionally bring her down in some way. But as he had experienced her so far, there had been no sign of this at all; and, it didn't really matter if she did. No one was perfect. But to laugh at one's own imperfections—as she had when the tomato jumped out of her hands—and to appreciate the imperfections of others, was simply another way of *choosing* to live that he had not considered before.

Searching his soul as he sat gently swinging, Brink knew with absolute certainty that even if he were to drive off tomorrow without Olivia, he would still feel what he was feeling in this moment at his core. Like the sun behind the clouds, this happiness was coming from a light *within* him, not from the apparent circumstances of the moment…including this beautiful creature sitting by his side watching the sun go down.

The glow from the sun almost paled in comparison to the glow coming from within him now. There would be no more covering up of his happiness any longer! He made a commitment to himself, right then and there, that he would keep that core of joy at the forefront, regardless of circumstances that might temporarily cloud over it.

As if she could sense Brink's ease, Olivia shifted a bit more and put her hand on his arm, leaning her weight just a bit more against him…still without saying a word. Brink was enjoying the feeling of her close presence, yet without feeling any need to continue casual conversation, allowing him to simply stay uninterrupted with his own train of thought.

He suddenly felt that he had an *ally* now…a powerful tool–a friend, actually–that he knew he could rely on for the rest of his days on this planet spinning through the universe. After all of his close to forty long and painful years, he felt that he had somehow awakened, becoming *conscious and aware* of the thinking that had been plaguing him…as if he had been living in a dream all this time! And in that waking up, he now had his moment to moment *awareness* of himself–the Watcher–on his side.

Sure…he somehow knew that he might slip back into sleep, so to speak, if he wasn't careful. But now he could keep that ally alongside him…that one who would be there as a *constant* to observe both his apparently 'good' and 'bad' moments, as he used to refer to them. He could see in this new lucid state that those values of good and bad that he had assigned to his experiences were really just a reflection of his pleasure or pain…either his clinging to or his pushing away from something.[12] He knew now that both of those were simply ways that he had built the world in his mind to hold on to something that he could call his own…his identity…his life…his *'Brinkness,'* one could even call it.

While it might appear to one observing from the outside that the happiness he was feeling in this moment was tied to Olivia, on a much deeper level he knew with certainty that the light emanating from within him would continue, regardless of her presence. And somehow–at the very same time as it radiated from within him–he was also *observing* this. The fact was that she *was* present at this moment…very much so. And the ease of being in silence with which she was there with him, and he with her, was one that didn't require constant words or conversation between them.

As his 'Watcher' continued to observe, what he saw was absolutely astounding. Earlier, in the garden, he had vividly seen how the clouds piling up–like the darkness of his thoughts–had obstructed the sun from shining through. Yet somehow even that was still just a two dimensional image. But now what he was truly *feeling*–not just thinking–was how the darkness of his emotions and repressed sadness over his father leaving had wrapped his heart from all sides. It was as if a ton of coal had dropped around him, choking him from every direction...until the darkness of that coal felt almost *comfortable*. His isolation from others, his ongoing depression and the constant suffocation of his very *life* was now–like a diamond formed from the pressure over time–ready to radiate into the world and sparkle! The joy coming from within him was a new and welcome feeling…a feeling of freedom beyond anything he had ever before imagined.

Somewhere in this newfound consciousness, Brink knew that most feelings eventually fade or morph into some other, not as welcome, emotion. What was growing within him was the awareness that–like a diamond with its many facets–this momentary euphoria was only one of many feelings that could change at any time…just as the clouds of his thoughts would continue to pass by.

His anger, sadness, fear and even shame, would more than likely surface again at points in his all too human lifetime. Yet he now knew that he could *watch* these feelings as they came and went. That was not to say that he would be so detached that he wouldn't actually *feel* them. What would be the point of living in this body of his and not utilizing its awesome senses? If he were completely detached and numb from their direct experience, he would actually be *missing out* on some of the greatest emotions and experiences his body and this experience of being human had to offer him! That would be like skydiving but not feeling the wind in his face...or eating Godiva chocolate but not tasting it!

Olivia shifted again, this time gently leaning her head against his shoulder, as Brink allowed his thoughts to continue to pass by him, watchfully.…

As he felt her head resting on his shoulder, he was convinced that this was what life at its fullest was most definitely about…feeling, experiencing, tasting, touching, crying, laughing and more. All of this beautiful variety of experiences awaited him! Brink felt his heart suddenly surge in lament for the loss of so many of the life experiences that he had not allowed himself to actually *feel*...like his dad leaving. He had never allowed himself to truly feel the sadness...to grieve...because he 'had to be a man' and not cry!

As his heart once again touched that tender place, he continued to simultaneously *notice and watch* from his own consciousness above. The watching allowed him to be *grateful* for his sadness...and for the sadness and deep grief to rise up and pass through him in a good way, rather than to stay stuck and buried in his heart, as the old Brink had done for so long.

There was a profound freedom that this watching brought him. And–even though his intuition told him that anger and fear would probably not visit him again for quite a while–he knew that if and when they did, his ally 'the Watcher' would be there once again to assist him in letting go of even those. The key was to simply *observe* the anger, the fear or whatever else might arise within him for what it was...and then to *relax and release* with the awareness of his Watcher.

Brink breathed in...then out again...slowly and deeply...relishing in the thought and feeling of his newfound awareness. In this watching, he actually *rose above himself* to notice and observe all that was arising in his mind and body in this very moment. As he watched the vividness of his internal processes from the vantage point of his own *observer*, he could simultaneously see and feel the beauty and vastness of the entire universe that lay before him. It was only by releasing the pain that had been stored within him that he now realized how he had been blocking himself by spending all of his conscious moments staring into his own inner psyche, rather than experiencing the richness of all of life instead.

He smiled to himself, as he saw clearly that there really was no such thing as 'positive' or 'negative' in all he had ever experienced; there was no drama and no problems except for those that he had created for himself in his own mind! In fact, with all that he had put himself through, he now saw that he wasn't even the sum of all of his experiences! Rather, the only real constant thread that existed was his *awareness* of the sum of those experiences. "He"–Brink–*was* merely the thread of consciousness itself that had the capacity to *observe* all of his experiences, both internal and external.

Suddenly, Brink could feel a bright, almost blinding, light radiating from within him as never before. It was as if a purification of his soul had taken place and the direction of his energy had been shifted from staring down into the depths of his psyche and out into the world to an upward release and pull of his spirit toward some higher, more profound level of being. There were simply no words to describe his presence in this moment, and a bubble of laughter and joy arose seemingly from nowhere...or perhaps from his suddenly being 'now-here.'[13]

As he stared into the dark night sky, with Olivia leaning up gently against him, in his mind's eye Brink could already see and feel the new day rising. In his vision the sun wasn't even peeking over the horizon yet, but its light was already illuminating the few scattered clouds that were floating silently above. Those closest to it were a bright white; those a bit further had a soft reddish glow rounding into the blue backdrop of the sky itself.

These were his thoughts and feelings being illuminated, reflecting off of one another in the playground of his mind and body. And in his mind, as he watched tomorrow morning's sun peek over the horizon, he could feel his new awareness rise with it…and the strength of his Watcher steadily grew. The light reflecting from the sun and this new conscious awareness created a subtle yet significant shift on the outline of his thoughts and feelings. His body shifted slightly and his mind squinted awake as he felt the steady light breeze in the air. There would be no more piling up of his thoughts or hanging onto them for Brink! Instead, only the beauty of being in the moment and experiencing its fullness would prevail. There was no going back to sleep now...simply a new day and a whole new life ahead of him! This was now his conscious *choice*–the decision to claim a new way of being for himself and to live with a newfound freedom as never before.

Olivia moved again, just a whisper closer to him…this time nuzzling her head deeper into his shoulder and bringing her hand up to rest on his chest….

He had only arrived here 24 hours ago. Yet somehow in just this short period of time the world had opened up for him in a way that he could never before fathom. If he could feel this good just by stepping out from the power of his own negative thoughts and self-criticisms, what might be possible if he actually consciously started focusing on his *positive* thoughts?   It seemed as if *anything* could probably materialize if he set his mind to it!

Right now, however–before allowing himself to spin off into the future–he chose instead to settle into the moment. Olivia had continued to nuzzle her head further into his shoulder, much in the way that he was now so used to Jackamo pushing up against him. It almost felt as if her head belonged there, had always been there, nestled peacefully into the dip between his chest and shoulder like a custom fit. He reached his arm around her shoulder and gently embraced her, feeling the warmth of her face melt into his body.

Just then, Jackamo jumped up on the swing on his other side and pushed the back of his little soft head against Brink's other hand…as always, looking for something to scratch himself against. Again he could feel the cat's cold nose, but this time it felt welcoming to him rather than a small nuisance, as it had the first time he experienced it.

Brink held his hand firm, so Jackamo could push against it with some resistance...business as usual for him. Then he wiggled his fingers in a circular, sporadic motion, as if typing on a keyboard. The cat pushed up against his fixed-in-position yet moving fingers, then rotated his head around them...first behind his ears, then under his neck, then back again around to the top of his head. He seemed so simply satisfied...so gentle and appreciative of Brink's willingness to serve as his living scratching post...purring with delight and gratitude.

When Jackamo had had enough, he settled down and his purring took on a steady rhythm...purr-two-three, purrr-two-three, purrrr-two-three. The purrs seemed to grow deeper and louder with each cycle. Brink noticed his own breathing fall in sync with the cat's rhythm, as his breath resonated deeper and deeper into his being.

Between the love coming through his hand resting on the cat's back and the love radiating from Olivia's head resting on his shoulder, the peace that he had been seeking for so long seemed suddenly–and simply– present. He could feel his heart open and his love reaching out, wrapping around Olivia and radiating through his arm to Jackamo. Equally as strong, he could feel the love embracing himself, *accepting himself,* in a way that was completely new for him.

In that moment, Brink's *Watcher* noticed both the outside love of others that he was finally letting in, and the peaceful and pure love emanating from within him flowing out to the world. In fact, there seemed to be no separation at all in that moment…all was one.

Olivia shifted just a bit, nuzzling against his shoulder, then whispered quietly to him, "Brink?"

"Yes, Olivia?"

"Come with me...there's one room in the house that I haven't had a chance to show you yet." Then she stood up, slipped her hand gently into his, opened the door with its already familiar creaking, and led him into the house and up the stairs….

[tHe bEgiNnIng]

Author's Comment

While no direct reference is made to it, I would be remiss if I did not mention and heartily recommend the "New Warrior Training Adventure" for any man 18 years of age or older to attend (including elder men well into their upper years). This two day, heart-opening experience is sponsored by The Mankind Project, a non-profit organization currently active in 32 states and a total of 14 countries throughout the world. More information can be found at: **www.MankindProject.org** (or **www.mkp.org**). There a man can find a list of communities and confidential, safe circles of men to visit as an introduction to this powerful transformational work. [Note: Women can find information on MKP's sister organization at www.WomanWithin.org]

Footnotes

[1] As referenced in <u>The Untethered Soul</u> by Michael A. Singer, Chapter 4 – The Lucid Self: "There is a type of dream, called a lucid dream, in which you know you're dreaming. You think, *"Hey, look! I'm dreaming that I'm flying. I'm going to fly over there."* You are actually conscious enough to know that you are flying in the dream and that you are dreaming the dream. That's very different from regular dreams, in which you are fully immersed in the dream."

[2] WHAT IS BURNING MAN?
http://www.burningman.com/whatisburningman/

Burning Man is an annual event and a thriving year-round culture. The event takes place the week leading up to and including Labor Day, in Nevada's Black Rock Desert. The Burning Man organization (Black Rock City LLC) creates the infrastructure of Black Rock City, wherein attendees (or "participants") dedicate themselves to the spirit of community, art, self-expression, and self-reliance. They depart one week later, leaving no trace. As simple as this may seem, trying to explain what Burning Man is to someone who has never been to the event is a bit like trying to explain what a particular color looks like to someone who is blind. In this section you will find the peripheral <u>definitions of what the event is</u> as a whole, but to truly understand this event, one must participate.

[3] A monologue from the play *Hamlet* by William Shakespeare
To be, or not to be, –that is the question:
Whether 'tis nobler in the mind to suffer

The slings and arrows of outrageous fortune,
Or to take arms against a sea of troubles,
And by opposing end them? –To die, to sleep–
No more; and by a sleep to say we end
The heartache, and the thousand natural shocks
That flesh is heir to, –'tis a consummation
Devoutly to be wish'd. To die, to sleep;
To sleep, perchance to dream: –ay, there's the rub; *[cont.]*
[Again, my thanks go out to Mickey Singer for his wonderful and inspiring talk at Christmas 2013 at the Temple of the Universe outside of Gainesville, FL. If you are ever in the area, don't miss the opportunity to go and hear him speak!]

[4] References taken from "Life Along the 100th Meridian", photo essay published December 6, 2013, NY Times Magazine, text by Inara Verzemnieks, featuring photo portfolio by Andrew Moore.

[5] Other emotions can typically be broken down into some variation or combination of these five core emotions. For example, 'anxiety' is a modified version of fear. This model is used by *The Mankind Project* in introducing men to the power of accessing their feelings.

[6]Shame v. Guilt distinction: "Although many people use these two words interchangeably, from a psychological perspective, they actually refer to different experiences. Guilt and shame sometimes go hand in hand; the same action may give rise to feelings of both shame and guilt, where the former reflects how we feel about *ourselves* and the latter involves an awareness that our actions have injured *someone else*. In other words, shame relates to

self, guilt to others. I think it's useful to preserve this distinction, even though the dictionary definitions often blur it…"   [Quoted from Joseph Burgo, Ph.D in his article "Shame – Toward Authentic Self-Esteem"]

[7] Laughter Yoga International is a "Global Movement for Health, Joy & World Peace". It was started in the early 90's by Indian medical Dr. Madan Kataria and currently has over 6000 practicing chapters worldwide. [Note: The Author, Z Newell, is a Certified Laughter Yoga Instructor.]

[8] The German word 'Geworfenheit' (translated 'Facticity') was the term philosopher Martin Heidegger coined in Zein und Zeit (Being and Time) as the starting point for examining our existence and finding meaning. This 'facticity' describes accepting the very *fact* of our existence as the starting point for discussion of the meaning of life, rather than the question of how we arrived here and whether or not there is a God. Many consider Heidegger to be the 'father of Existentialism' for this distinction, which resulted in a shift away from the nature of religion as the central focus for finding meaning in our daily existence. [Note: This is the author's interpretation from his own studies during time spent in Northwestern University's Philosophy PhD Program).

[9] Supercoach Michael Neill has built an entire coaching strategy and awareness around this concept. Refer to his newest book, The Inside-Out Revolution: The Only Thing You Need to Know to Change Your Life Forever

[10]Michael Singer, in his description of this yogic practice, refers to this as the 'seat of self'. The author highly recommends his audio CD entitled "The Clarity of Witness Consciousness" Part 1: The World, the Mind, the Heart, and You Part 2: Beyond the Pull of Inner Energies [available through Temple of the Universe online store at www.tou.org]

[11]Jelaluddin Rumi - 13th century mystic poet

DON'T GO BACK TO SLEEP

(also referred to as THE BREEZE AT DAWN)

The breeze at dawn has secrets to tell you.
Don't go back to sleep.
You must ask for what you really want.
Don't go back to sleep.
People are going back and forth across the doorsill
where the two worlds touch.
The door is round and open.
Don't go back to sleep.

~Rumi

[12]Eckhart Tolle, in The Power of Now, (as well as any look at the concept of 'detachment' in Buddhism), describes how the nature of pain comes from our separation from what he have either *lost* or *desire to have.*

[13]This term taken from Wayne Dyer's Your Sacred Self: Making the Decision to Be Free

~ Dear Friend ~

Thanks for reading
BRINK: Don't Go Back to Sleep
Please take a few minutes to rate or review this book on Amazon, post something on your Facebook wall, or share this gift of allegory in some way.

For more thoughts on a life of awakening from what lies beneath the surface
–and on creating a magnificent life for yourself–
please visit Z Newell's blog at:

WhatMadeMeThink.com

p.s. - You can also reach the author there for comments, feedback *or to submit a brief review of this book for publication in future editions.* Or simply email your review or comments to:
Z@WhatMadeMeThink.com.
Much appreciated!

~Z

ABOUT THE AUTHOR

"I co-create a vibrant world by inspiring
people's magnificence."

Ivan 'Z' Newell lives in Lexington, Kentucky with his wife to be Liz Haeberlin (photographer, writer, life coach), their cat Jackamo, and dogs Maggie & Mango. Lexington–in the heart of Bluegrass Country with its beautiful pastoral setting, thoroughbred horses, history and bourbon–is also known as the "Horse Capital of the World." This is Z's first novel. It is a blend of perspectives from his background in philosophy, psychology, over a decade of experience in transformational men's work, and his personal spiritual journey.

email: Z@WhatMadeMeThink.com

Made in the USA
Charleston, SC
14 July 2015